SAVAGE town

Savage Angels MC Series Book Three

Kathleen Kelly

Savage Town
Savage Angels MC Series Book Three

Kathleen Kelly

This book is a work of fiction. Any references to real events, real people, and real places are used fictitiously. Other names, characters, places and incidents are products of the Author's imagination and any resemblance to persons, living or dead, actual events, organizations or places is entirely coincidental.

All rights are reserved. This book is intended for the purchaser of this book ONLY. No part of this book may be reproduced or transmitted in any form or by any means, graphic, electronic, or mechanical, including photocopying, recording, taping, or by any information storage retrieval system, without the express written permission of the Author. All songs, song titles and lyrics contained in this book are the property of the respective songwriters and copyright holders.

All efforts have been made to ensure the correct grammar and punctuation in the book. If you do find any errors, please e-mail Kathleen Kelly: kathleenkellyauthor@gmail.com
Thank you.

Disclaimer: The material in this book contains graphic language and sexual content and is intended for mature audiences, ages 18 and older.

ISBN: 979-8401968289

Re-editing by Swish Design & Editing
Proofreading by Swish Design & Editing
Book design by Swish Design & Editing
Cover design by Clarise Tan at CT Cover Creations
Cover Image Copyright
First Edition 2015
Second Edition 2021
Copyright © 2021 Kathleen Kelly
All Rights Reserved

DEDICATION

To all the bloggers out there, you know who you are. Without your support and promotion, no one would know who I am or buy my books. Thank you from the bottom of my heart.
You keep this industry going, and you keep us authors in business.
Without you, we would all be lost.

SAVAGE *town*

CHAPTER 1

DANE
President Savage Angels MC

I hold my woman's hand as I burn her beautiful face into my memory. She's wearing more makeup than normal. She doesn't need it, but it will look good in the press photos. Her simple ivory wedding dress clings to her curves in a I-want-to-fuck-you-now kind of way. I look down at her fingers with my rings on them—a square-cut solitaire diamond set in gold with a wedding band having six smaller square-cut diamonds set into it. It's a little over the top, but she likes pretty things. As I turn her hand over, I notice a speck of red, I brush it away, and it smears across her palm.

My eyes travel to the lace covering her neck and over her shoulders where the material hides her scar. Sometimes it makes her self-conscious, but I don't think she needs to cover it. The bodice of her dress has tiny beads sewn onto it. They catch in the light, and as I stare at them, I notice the ivory turn red, and Kat jerks violently.

"Dammit! Sir, I need you to move, and I need you to do it now!" The paramedic pushes me, and I fall against the ambulance doors as it speeds toward the hospital. He grabs the scissors and cuts into the fabric of Kat's dress, exposing her lingerie, which she told me I'd appreciate later tonight.

I'm staring at the only woman I've ever loved as he tries to save her life. Looking at my hands, they have her blood all over them. I don't know what to do. How to help.

"Floor it, man! She's coding, we missed a fucking bullet wound! If we don't get there soon, she won't make it!" His eyes find mine, and he quickly looks away.

"Not going to fucking happen! You fucking *hear* me? You keep her here with *me*, got it?" I growl at him.

He nods repeatedly as he tends to her, his hands a blur as he applies gauze and pressure to Kat's small broken frame. Sweat beads on his upper lip as curse words spill from his mouth.

I'm on my knees in the back of the ambulance when suddenly the regular beeping noise of Kat's heart turns into one continuous beep.

CHAPTER 1

KAT

Two Weeks Earlier

It's two weeks before the wedding, and there's still so much to do! I've been around the MC long enough to know Dane is making a huge compromise by having a traditional wedding. It's not something the club normally does, but I wanted a fairy-tale wedding, and he's giving it to me. The reception is being held in Tourmaline's Town Hall. We've invited just about the entire town to make up for the disruption to their lives. The press questions and harasses everyone we have ever spoken to, so the invites are to try and keep on the town's good side.

"Kat, are you listening?" asks the town mayor, Justice Leaverton.

"Sorry, Justice, miles away. You were saying?"

"We have no problem with you having your reception here, but the concern is it's not big enough." I feel myself frown, and as I take in a deep breath to give him a piece of my mind, he raises both hands and continues. "All we're suggesting is you also take over the park in front of the hall. You can put up a marquee there and add more tables."

"For a moment, I thought you were going to cancel on me!"

"As if I'd do that to you. Besides, your future husband would probably string me up." He flashes his gorgeous smile.

Justice is six foot five, built, and has model good looks. Most of the women in town swoon whenever he enters a room, but I've come to call him a friend and a business associate.

"Don't use your smile on me." I try to use a stern voice but fail. "And you're right, Dane would string you up." He chuckles. "Thank you for the suggestion. A marquee is a great idea. I was going to try to make everyone fit into the hall, and it wasn't going to be pretty." I look up at him.

"Happy to help, and so are most of the locals. You're good for business, Kat." He grabs me by the elbow and guides me toward the park.

"I'm surprised they haven't tried to evict me by now. It's not only all the guests, but it is all the crazies, too."

"I've noticed your security detail has gotten bigger." He gestures toward my four bodyguards, courtesy of the Savage Angels MC. "They don't look happy, though."

As I stare at them, Dirt turns around and frowns at me, then gives Judge a nod in my direction. Judge says something to him, and the others laugh, then he walks toward us. He's six foot two and has a way of making you feel you're the only woman on the planet. Over the last couple of years, he's been my unofficial bodyguard, but with all the new people in town, Dane got him to pick three more of the brothers to look after me.

As he gets closer, he gives Justice a chin lift and places his arm around my shoulders. "Kat, sugar, you ready to roll?" He looks over at the brothers and says, "Dirt's had enough for today. If you don't feed us soon, he may bite someone."

"There's too much to do before the big day! Judge, can't you tell them I'll meet them at Bettie's Café? I only need to go over a couple more things, and then I need to talk to Adelynn at The Country Inn."

"No can do, sugar, Dane wouldn't like it, and he's been a tad aggressive lately."

"Judge is right, Kat, too many unfamiliar faces in Tourmaline for you to be walking around by yourself."

And as Justice finishes speaking, a reporter takes

a photo of me with Judge's arm around my shoulders. Judge takes two steps toward the photographer and grabs him by his shirt.

"Delete the photo now, or I'm going to help, and it looks like a *really* expensive-fucking-camera, which I'd hate to drop."

"You can't do that! Freedom of the Press!" the photographer yells.

"Fucker, you only took it to cause a problem with myself and the president of my MC, and I'm *not* going to let that happen. *Delete. It. Now.*" Judge leans into the frazzled-looking photographer as Dirt and the others surround him.

He would have to be my favorite MC member to hang out with, but it's times like this I understand why Dane put him in charge of me. He's gone from nice guy to I'm-going-to-put-my-fist-through-the-back-of-your-head in the blink of an eye. He can be deadly, and sometimes I forget how dangerous he can be.

"Judge," I place my hand on his arm. "This nice man *is* going to delete the photos, aren't you, honey?"

The photographer looks from me to Judge, then realizes he's surrounded by three more of the Savage Angels and the town mayor.

"Sure, sure, if you'll let me go, so I can do it?" Judge shoves him backward into Dirt, who pushes him forward.

The photographer pushes buttons, then finally says, "It's done!"

"Now, you don't think I'm going to take your word for it, *do* you?" says Judge. He takes the camera out of his hands and gives it to me. I go through the images, and there's a stack of me on there, but none with Judge's arm around my shoulders.

"It's fine. You can let him go," I say with a smile as I pass the camera back.

Judge takes a step back and says, "Enjoy your time in Tourmaline and remember to be respectful of all our citizens." He's back to being the joker as everyone laughs, but the photographer isn't falling for it. He slowly makes his way around Judge, not breaking eye contact, and walks backward until he's a good twelve feet away, then he turns and runs down the sidewalk.

"Judge, that wasn't really necessary," I say.

"Judge was right. Dane would've had a major fucking fit if he'd seen a picture of you two looking all cozy plastered across the front of some stupid-fucking-magazine or television. And, Judge, what the fuck were you thinking putting your arm around Kat in the first place? Brother, use your head." Dirt looks pissed, and the smile on Judge's face disappears. This could easily turn ugly if I don't intervene.

"Okay! Time out. I'm starving. Let's all go get

lunch, and I promise, no more wedding stuff today!"

Judge glances at me, then back at Dirt. "Sugar, we *both* know you have to see Addy, and there are probably a few other things you need to do today."

I step in between both men, holding my hands up just in case. "Yes, I do, but let's do lunch, then I'll re-evaluate what I need to do today, okay?"

"So *more*-fucking-wedding stuff?" Dirt mumbles, but when I look at him, he has a small smile on his lips.

"Yes, I lied, more-*fucking*-wedding stuff." The group of men laugh, and I turn to face the mayor. "Do you have a marquee big enough to cover the park?"

"Yes, we do, Kat. Are you happy to let us put it up? We even have flooring to cover the grass if you'd like?"

"Thank you so much, Justice." I grab his hand. "You saved me! I don't suppose you have tables and chairs, too?"

"Yes, we do, Kat, for a fee." He uses his smile on me again. Of course, there's a charge.

"Now, Justice, you better give me a discount, but I'm happy to pay! Can I forward your details to the wedding organizer so that he can finalize everything with you?"

"Absolutely. Now, go and enjoy your lunch." He nods at the brothers. "Gentlemen, you have fun now."

Justice chuckles and moves back into the Town Hall. I turn around and link my arm through Judge's and take my group of bodyguards to Bettie's Café.

"Hey, Kat!" yells the lovely Rosie, our server at Bettie's.

"Hey, Rosie, what's good today?"

"It's all good, Kat." She leans in and quietly says, "But I'd avoid the house special today." She gives me a wink and goes off to pour coffee for the other patrons.

"Oh my God! You're Kat Saunders!" A young girl screams as she runs across the room toward me.

Judge takes his position in front of me and grabs her as she gets close. "Sorry, sugar, but you're close enough."

"But it's Kat Saunders! She's really here!" She screams again, trying to get around an immovable Judge.

"Judge, it's okay."

"No, Kat, it isn't. Rosie! Can we order and have it delivered to the compound, please, sugar?"

"Yes, Judge. Shall I do up your usual orders?"

He gives her a thumbs up and looks at Dirt. "You

want to escort Kat back to the compound? I'll only be a minute."

Dirt grabs my arm and drags me out of Bettie's.

"Dirt, this isn't necessary! She's only a fan!" I try to pull my arm out of his grasp, but he holds on tighter.

"If she were *only* a fan, do you think Judge would've done what he did? How long has he been looking after you? Do you really think he'd do that if she were *just* a fan?"

He continues to walk me down the sidewalk. "Okay, okay, can you let me go?"

I know he's right. Judge has been around long enough to know the difference between a fan and a crazy. I don't enjoy being manhandled or told what to do. As I'm about to tell him this, my phone rings. It's seriously bad timing.

"Hello?" There's breathing on the end of the line. "Hello? Anyone there?"

"Kat?"

"This is she. Who's this?"

"Kat, it's Gareth."

I stop walking. Hell, I think I stop breathing. Dirt takes one look at my face and snatches my phone out of my hand.

"Who's this?" he growls into the phone. He turns, so I'm staring at his back. "Hold up, fucker, this isn't Dane. You ring this number again, and I'll find you, and you won't like it. We clear?" He turns back around and is holding the phone out to me. I stand there like an idiot, staring at it. "Kat?"

"It was Gareth. How did Gareth get my number?"

"Fucker!" He puts the phone in his pocket. Then he embraces me and nearly squeezes the life out of me. "He's still in the nuthouse, yeah? So, he can't get to you. We'll keep you safe." He pulls away from me, grips me by my shoulders, and gazes into my eyes. "We *will* sort this out."

"Dirt, you want to explain why you're hugging my woman on Main Street?" asks Dane.

I look behind Dirt, and there he is, my future husband, and I launch myself into his arms.

"Whoa, darlin', what gives?"

"Gareth-fucking-Goodman just called her phone."

I'm shaking, and I can feel Dane stiffen at Gareth's name.

"How the fuck did he get her number?" growls Dane.

"I've no fucking idea, brother, but we'll find out," says Dirt.

Dane takes a step back from me and clasps my face in his hands. "Come on, darlin', let's get you back to the compound. I'll need you to write down everyone you have given your number to. We'll get it sorted." He brushes his lips against mine. "Come on." He puts his arm around my shoulders. "Tell me what you've accomplished for the wedding today?"

"Like you really care."

He feigns looking hurt, but a smile plays on his lips. "Of course, I care."

"You only care if I actually make you do anything. Which reminds me, have you finalized the suits yet?"

"Did I agree to a suit?"

"Dane Reynolds! You *know* you did!" I know he's trying to get my mind off Gareth as I watch a mischievous smile spread across his face.

"You must have gotten me at a weak moment and used your feminine wiles on me."

"Feminine wiles? Seriously?"

"You're not accusing me—"

A scream pierces the air, and we turn around to see Judge trying to keep a crowd of fans at bay.

"Dirt, brothers, go help Judge. I'll take Kat back to the compound." His voice oozes authority.

He grabs my hand and marches me back to the compound. When we're inside the gates, he whistles and does the signal in the air to shut them.

"Darlin', don't take this the wrong way, but I'll be glad when this is all-fucking-over. I will be glad when my town goes back to normal." He pulls me into a tight embrace.

"It's only two more weeks, and then you'll have me forever. I told you when we first met, your life was going to be turned upside down. It's all part and parcel of being famous."

He kisses me, and I feel it to my core. "I don't like it. I don't like all the strangers in town, and I don't like Gareth-*fucking*-Goodman phoning you. Let's get a list written up and go through it. See who might have slipped it to him." He looks grim as his blue eyes flash with anger.

"You promised once to keep me safe." I step out of his embrace and start walking backward, teasing him. "In fact, you said all I needed to do was call *savage,* and you'd come running." I turn and run toward the clubhouse. "Savage!"

Before I can make it to the steps, he wraps his arms around my waist and throws me over his shoulder, slapping my ass. My laughter fills the clubhouse as he carries me through to our room and throws me on the bed.

"Now, who's going to keep you safe from me, darlin'?"

"Oh, you won't hurt me."

"No?"

"No. You love me, Dane Reynolds. You've proven it just about every day since we've met. Now, let me prove it to you."

He chuckles while undoing his belt. He has the top button of his jeans undone when a loud knock sounds on the door.

"Fuck," he murmurs as he turns around and throws open the door. "What?"

"Hey, Prez, need to talk. It's been a while."

Standing on the other side of the door is Kade. He's a nomad, but he's been spending more and more time around Tourmaline. He is well-liked within the club and has become Fith's unofficial replacement since he went missing.

"Kade, what brings you back to Tourmaline?"

"Might have a lead on the loft Fith mentioned."

I laugh, and both men turn to me with serious looks on their faces. "Fith and the loft?" I chuckle.

"Darlin', this is serious club business. Mind if we pick this up later?"

"Sure, I'll write a list now."

He nods, comes over to the bed, kisses me, and then does up his jeans and belt. "See you tonight."

As they close the door, I hear Kade mention the loft again. I wonder if Fith told him what it stands for before he left town.

CHAPTER 2

SHERIFF CARLOS MORALES

The walls of my office seem to be closing in on me as I listen to the detective on the other end of my phone. Katarina Saunders might be good for the local economy, and I might really like her, but with the influx of new people in my town, crime is up, and my small police force isn't big enough to handle it. There's been nothing serious, vandalism and the odd drunken fight, but it's been every day or night for the past month. The sooner the wedding of the year is over and done with, the better off my town will be.

"Sheriff, you still there?"

"Yes, detective. How the hell did this happen?"

"Looks like he had outside help. We're still looking into it. Can you inform Ms. Saunders?"

"Of course, detective. Is there anything else I should know?"

"I looked at his room. He had photos of her everywhere. She needs to be careful."

"How the fuck did he get pictures of her?" Irritation colors my tone.

His sigh echoes over the phone. "They're mostly magazine pictures, but there are a couple which is actual photos. He has a lot of fans."

"Do you think he's headed here?"

"Not sure, but he has an unhealthy obsession with her. Apparently, they were working through it in therapy. Look, Sheriff, we don't know anything yet, but I'll keep you in the loop."

"Thank you, detective. Have a nice day." I hang up and stare at the phone. "Yeah, have a nice-fucking-day." *Un-fucking-believable. Gareth-fucking-Goodman has escaped from Willowbrook Psychiatric Hospital. Can this day get any worse?*

There's a knock at my door, and Deputy Billy Barrett is standing there. "Come in, deputy."

"Sheriff, Adelynn at The Country Inn just called. There's some kind of disturbance in one of her rooms, and she asked if you'd come look. I could go if you'd like?"

I like Deputy Barrett well enough. Never been able to confirm he's on the take with the Savage Angels MC, though. I know he has ties to them, so I keep him on a short leash, just the same.

"No, I'll go. Get your gear, deputy. You can come, too. Just in case it's more than I can handle, though I doubt it." With a sigh, I stand, put my gun in my holster, and grab my hat.

"Okay, Sheriff, I'm on it. We walking or driving?"

"Today we drive. I have other business to attend to as well."

He gets the keys to my cruiser as I head toward the front door. It's another beautiful day in Tourmaline. The sun is out, and it's not too hot. I look up at the blue sky and put my sunglasses on as Deputy Barrett hits the sidewalk.

"You can drive, deputy."

"Yes, Sheriff."

He's learned over the last couple of years that I don't tolerate small talk. Not unless we're dating, and Deputy Barrett isn't my type. The only person I sort of date in this town is Adelynn—Addy—at The Country Inn. I like her more than a little, but she's made it perfectly clear, she's hooked on the VP of the Savage Angels MC, Jonas. Can't understand it myself. She's a good woman, and he left her without so much as a goodbye.

She has a son, Ben, from her late husband. He's a great kid, and we get along well. I keep hoping Addy will see I'm the better choice, but as yet, I haven't been able to break through.

When we pull into the parking lot of The Country Inn, shouts can be heard coming from a room. Addy comes out of the office, and I point at the door, questioning if it's the correct one. She nods, and I give her a two-fingered wave.

"Okay, deputy, go knock on the door, and we'll see how well you handle this one."

"On it, Sheriff."

Walking up to the door, he does a double knock, then takes two steps back and to the side. He's been trained well, even had him and two of my other men do a course in hostage negotiation at Quantico. The government gives me funding every year to train my men, unlike some of the other sheriffs in neighboring counties, and I use it. You never know when it's going to come in handy. I'm sending another deputy to learn how to disable bombs next month.

The door gets thrown open. "What?" says a disheveled-looking man standing in the doorway.

"Good afternoon, sir. I'm Deputy Barrett from the Tourmaline Sheriff's Office. There have been—"

"What do you want?" yells the man.

"I want you to step outside, lower your voice, and answer a few questions."

I'm impressed. He's made a show of putting his hand on his gun and is using a more authoritative tone. The man seems to respond well by doing what he's told.

"Sorry, officer, it's just that—"

"Do you have any identification on you, sir?" Deputy Barrett is quick to interrupt, keeping control of the situation.

"Deputy Barrett, I'm sorry. It's my girlfriend, and she's being... difficult." The man hands over his driver's license, and it appears as though my deputy has it under control, so I head over to the office to see Addy.

Before I knock on the door, she opens it. "Hey Carlos, thank you so much for coming."

"Hello, Addy." I look over my shoulder at Deputy Barrett and say, "Billy looks like he has it under control."

"Yes, he does. They've been going at it for an hour. I thought maybe they'd calm down, but it seemed to be escalating."

"You should've called me as soon as it got loud." I look back at Addy. "You want to get dinner later tonight?"

"That would be great, Carlos. My dad has an AA meeting at five thirty, so how does seven sound? Then he can look after Ben."

"How about I pick you up at six, and Ben comes with us?"

She looks at her shoes, and I know she's weighing it up. I know she doesn't want Ben to get used to me in case we don't work out, but I think two years of taking it slow is enough. Moving into her, I touch her face.

"Carlos, you know how I feel about you, *you know*." Her eyes come up to meet mine.

"I know, Addy, but he's not going to come back to you. Jonas might be back in town, but he hasn't so much as called you, has he? I'd never treat you like he did."

She reaches up to hold my hand to her face. "I know, Carlos."

"Ahh, Sheriff?" Deputy Barrett says from behind me.

I sigh and let go of Addy and turn around. "Yes, Billy?"

He seems surprised I've used his name, and for a moment, he stares at me. "The gentleman has calmed down, and I have convinced him, he and his girlfriend should leave town." He looks at Addy. "Sorry, Addy, he said he's paid up to the end of the week, but they aren't good for each other, and the sooner they leave town, the better."

"Excellent work, Billy. Do we need to wait around, or will he leave peacefully?" I ask.

"He shouldn't be any trouble now, Sheriff. If it's all right with you, I'll wait until they've gone."

"Thanks, Billy. I have to go down to the Savage Angels compound and see Dane. You sure you're all right?" I ask.

"Yes, Sheriff, I have it all under control." He grins at me, clearly pleased with himself.

I turn back around and look at Addy. "Well, I'm

off, then. See you tonight?"

"Actually, Carlos, I mean Sheriff, I need to talk to one of the guys in the garage about my ice machine. Could I come with you?" asks Addy.

"Of course, it would be my pleasure."

The smile on her face grows, and she says, "I need to tell Dad where I'm going. I'll only be a sec."

I watch as she goes inside, and I nod at Deputy Barrett and head for the cruiser. Opening the passenger side door, I wait for her. She waves at her dad and Billy as she makes her way to me. Addy is five foot ten with long brown hair. She's easily the best-looking woman in Tourmaline. She grew up here but married an army man and only moved back after he died. I know she's had a few troubles with her dad, but he seems to have sorted himself out now. She loved her husband, and it's another reason I've taken it slow with her, but I'm about to take this to another level, having dinner with her, and Ben should tell her that.

"My lady," I say as I help her into the cruiser. She laughs and does her seat belt.

As I get into the cruiser, she says, "Why are you going to see Dane?"

"This wedding is going to be the end of me. Just need to go over security for Kat and see if he needs any help."

Lying to her doesn't sit well with me, but I don't want her to worry about Gareth Goodman. She has a full motel and is also helping Kat with extra guests at Dane's place. He has five cottages built on his property along with the main house, and they're going to be full of wedding guests. She's offered to help cater and look after them.

When we drive through the gates of the compound, I get out and open Addy's door.

"You going to be all right dealing with the guys?" She knows I mean Jonas.

A smile plays at her lips. "Yes, Carlos, I'm going to be *fine*."

"Good."

Before she has time to react, I lean in and kiss her lightly on the lips, smile at her, and head into the clubhouse. Out of the corner of my eye, I see Jonas watching from the garage office, and I want him to know Addy isn't his anymore.

Bear comes to meet me just inside the clubhouse doors. "Afternoon, Sheriff."

"Bear, is Dane or Kat around?" I ask.

"Dane is in a meeting. Would you mind waiting while I go get him?"

"Take your time."

He's a huge guy and one of the nicest members of the MC. He walks to their meeting room, knocks once, then opens the door. I can't hear what he's saying, but his head is nodding in the affirmative. The door swings wide, and Dane Reynolds comes out. The guy is six foot six and built like a linebacker.

"Sheriff, what can I do for you?" says Dane.

Our relationship has been tenuous since the troubles with his sister, Emily. I'm sure they killed the man who abducted her, but I have no proof. I've kept the MC under a microscope since then, busting them for things like noise complaints to lewd behavior. Amazingly, I have a good rapport with Kat, she and I are firm friends. Kat doesn't let my dealings with her husband interfere with our friendship. In fact, I think it amuses her.

"Dane, is Kat around? I'd like to talk to both of you together."

He frowns at me and says, "Okay, Sheriff, let me go get her. Take a seat, I'll only be a sec."

I make my way to the bar and lean up against it. Rebel is serving drinks, and a couple of the MC stand around drinking. I look at them, and they move away from me. Rebel gives me a chin lift.

"Rebel, how are things?"

"Things would be better, Sheriff, if your boys would stop harassing me every chance they get. Can't ride from one side of town to the other without one of them pulling me over and checking my license and registration."

He puts both hands on the bar and leans toward me. Under my direction, my men, every couple of months, harass him. He betrayed me. No, he used me, so he and his MC could exact their own kind of justice on those who hurt Emily Reynolds.

"Now, Rebel, my men are only doing their jobs, but I'll tell them to lay off. How does that sound?"

"I'd appreciate any help you could give me." He looks as serious as he sounds. Maybe next time, he'll think twice before he screws me over.

"Carlos!" It's Kat's bubbly voice, making me turn around. She walks toward me and hugs me. "What are you doing here?"

"Kat, is there somewhere more private we can talk?" I smile at her but look up at Dane.

"Babe, can we use the meeting room?" she asks Dane.

"I'll ask Kade to vacate," he says.

She smiles at him as he walks past us, but she hasn't taken her eyes off me. "So, did I see you kiss Adelynn outside? Something you want to share?"

I chuckle at her. "No, Kat, nothing I'd like to share."

Kat links her arm through mine and guides me toward the meeting room.

"Carlos, you're no fun! I'm about to become an old married lady, and I need to live vicariously through you, so spill!"

"Kat, you are many things, but I don't think you'll ever be an old lady, even when you're ninety. Something tells me you'll always be young at heart." She bursts out laughing. "And really nosey."

"Carlos!" Kat hits me on the arm. "I can't believe

you said that!"

I put my hands up, palms facing her. "Okay, okay, maybe I went too far with the young-at-heart thing."

I duck as she tries to hit me again, and Dane engulfs her in a bear hug from behind.

"Now, darlin', I don't need the sheriff putting you in jail for assault. After all, it's been an entire week since one of us has been arrested for some bogus charge."

"Now, Dane, you and I both know your boys only get arrested if they break the law."

All humor leaves my voice, and Dane and I stare at each other, not breaking eye contact.

"Enough, you two!" says Kat, twisting to look up at Dane. "Is the meeting room free?"

"Yes, darlin', the meeting room is free."

They both go into the room, and I follow. Kat sits down at the head of the table, and Dane looks at her, shaking his head.

Kat gives him her biggest smile and says, "So, what's up, Carlos?"

"Ahh, Dane, could you sit, too?" I ask.

He raises both eyebrows at me, then goes and sits on the other side of Kat.

"I need you to know I have asked the other sheriffs in neighboring counties to lend me some of their men in the coming weeks. Even the state troopers have offered some reinforcements."

"Carlos, I'm so sorry our wedding is causing you such a headache. Can we do anything to make your life easier?" asks Kat.

"No, Kat, you aren't any trouble. I'm telling you all this, as I want you to know you're safe. I'm doing everything in my power to keep you that way."

She nods and looks at Dane, but he's staring at me. "Sheriff, why are you here?"

I look at him, then turn to face Kat. "Gareth Goodman escaped from the psychiatric hospital he was in yesterday."

Kat's face goes pale, and Dane immediately puts his arm around her shoulders. "Mother-fucking-asshole." He turns her face toward him. "Kat, I left your phone in our room. Can you go get it, and have you done up the list?" Kat stands and hurries out of the room. When she's across the far side of the clubhouse, he says, "He called her today."

"Why didn't you tell me?"

"I thought he was still in custody. I thought he was trying to wreck our wedding day. I didn't know he was fucking out and might try to get to my woman." His voice has gone cold and steely as his eyes flash with anger.

"How did he get her number?" I ask.

"We don't know. I asked Kat to write down everyone she has given her number to recently. Do you think he'll come after her?" Dane places his arms on the table and leans forward. "Sheriff, is my woman in danger?"

"According to the detective on the case, he has a shrine built for Kat, and they were..." I use my fingers as inverted commas, "... working through it in therapy."

"He has a shrine built for me? How did he get my picture?" Kat asks from behind me.

I turn around to stare at her. "Most of them are from magazines, but some are the real deal. He may have someone in town feeding him information, or it could just be a fan. Either way, you need to be more careful. They don't think he'd come here, but no one suspected him before. Look at all the women who came forward after he was arrested. He's smart, so we'll have to be smarter."

She nods and holds out her phone and a piece of paper to me. "Obviously, everyone in my phone has my number, but these are the people I can think of that I have *recently* given my number to."

I take both of them off her. "Just keep doing what you would normally do." I look at Dane. "You've got more men on her now, don't you?"

"Yes, I do. It was only Judge, but I increased her detail to four brothers. Do you think it's enough?"

"We have no evidence to suggest he's on his way here. Four should be plenty." I turn to face Kat. "What exactly did he say to you, Kat?"

"All he really said was hello and that it was him. Dirt took my phone and did most of the talking." Kat walks to Dane, who, as soon as she gets within reaching distance, pulls her into his frame. I might not like him and his MC, but there's no denying he loves Kat and will do anything to protect her.

"I'll need to talk to Dirt. Can you find him for me?" I ask.

Dane kisses the top of her head. "Kat, darlin', wait here with Carlos while I go find him in the garage."

"Dane, would you mind telling Addy I'm going to be a little while? She's in the garage talking to one of your mechanics about her ice machine. Don't want her waiting around for me if she has business to attend to."

"Not a problem, I'll be back." He kisses the top of Kat's head and walks toward the front of the clubhouse.

CHAPTER 3

JONAS
VP Savage Angels MC

I watched as the fucking sheriff opened his passenger door and helped Addy get out. Then the fucker kissed her and smiled. If I thought I was over her, seeing that proved I wasn't. An angry growl escapes my lips and I break the pencil I'm holding in half. The thing is, I know I fucked it up between us, and I know she's been seeing him for a while, but I've never seen them together. Addy watches him go into the clubhouse, then walks toward the office where I happen to be. I've always enjoyed watching her walk—she's tall and does it with confidence. Today she's wearing a skirt that hugs her long legs as she moves.

I move from behind my desk and lean against the

front of it. I have my feet crossed at the ankles and my arms folded across my chest. The windows to the office are tinted, so she can't see me, but I see her. When she reaches the door to the office, she knocks once, then opens it.

"Oh! Jonas? How... I mean, well, how are you?"

Good, I've made her nervous.

"I'm good, Addy. Didn't realize you and the sheriff had gotten so close. Guess you've moved on." I am more than angry, and I know I don't have a right to be, but she's the only woman I'd even consider making room for in my life. When Ray got killed, it changed everything, except for the way I feel about her.

"I beg your pardon?"

"I said you and the sheriff seem very cozy. How does Ben like him?"

"What? How dare you!" She shakes her head, throws her arms up in the air, and turns to leave, but before I even know what I'm doing, I'm across the room, slamming the door shut. I have both my arms on either side of her as she turns around. "Get away from me!" she hisses.

"Do you like it when he kisses you, Addy? Do you like it better than me?" Before she can answer, I clasp her face and press my lips to hers as my hands travel down her body. She tries to push me away, but as I grab her ass and grind into her, she whimpers. Picking her up, I walk toward my desk, putting her ass on it. I spread her legs as my hands cup her breasts, and my thumbs rub over her erect nipples. Wrapping her legs around me, Addy kisses me back.

I stop to take a step back and look at her, lips swollen, eyes full of desire. "Tell me, Addy, can he make you feel like I just made you feel?" I whisper.

"Bastard!" She pushes me away and runs for the door, but I grab her arm, stopping her.

"You'll always belong to me, Addy. It's the same for me."

"He wouldn't walk out on me without an explanation! He wouldn't make me feel like a whore!" Addy hisses again.

"No, love, you aren't a whore, but you *are* mine." I let her go, and she walks back toward the door, shaking her head from side to side.

"It's been over three years, Jonas, and nothing. Not a word from you. Now I'm finally seeing a man, a good man, and you want me back?" I give her a slight nod. "It's too late. You're too late!"

"If it were too late, love, you wouldn't have kissed me back, you wouldn't have let me get between your legs just now, and we both know you wouldn't have stopped me if I'd kept going." I take a step toward her, and she takes a step back.

She still shakes her head, staring at me disbelievingly. "No, it's been a long time. I was simply overcome. I—"

"It's been a long time?" I let out a laugh. "You haven't fucked him yet, have you, Addy?"

"That's none of *your* concern. You made it *perfectly* clear all those years ago."

"I fucked up, love, and I'm sorry." I close the gap between us and clasp her face in my hands. "What if we start again? This time I'm not going anywhere. Tell me you'll give me another chance. Tell me it's not too late, Addy."

Addy puts her forehead to mine. "Carlos is a good man, and Ben does like him."

"What's going on between you and me has nothing to do with Carlos. I'll talk to him, I'll sort it out. All you have to say is you're willing to give me a second chance, and I promise you, love, I won't fuck it up again."

She pulls back from me. "No, I'm having dinner with Carlos tonight. I can—"

"No, love, I can see you aren't getting this. There's *no more* Carlos. If you and I are going to give this another shot, Carlos has to go, and he has to go today. Right now."

"I need time. You can't start telling me what to do. I don't even *know* if I want this!"

"Love, *you* want this, or you would've fucked the sheriff by now."

Her eyebrows come together, and she looks at me quizzically.

"You hurt me, Jonas. How can I trust you aren't

going to go off again? How can I let you have a relationship with my son when I don't even trust you to be here next week?"

"We'll take it slow. I'll earn your trust back somehow. Addy, you still care for me, can't you please, love, give me another chance?"

Her eyes search mine. "I need to be the one to talk to Carlos. I owe him that much."

"Addy, I—"

"No, Jonas. Carlos is a good man, and he deserves to hear it from me."

"Trust me when I tell you, Carlos will understand it better if it comes from me. Can you do that?"

Slowly she nods, and I clasp her face in my hands. Even with Addy's height, I'm six foot six, so I tower over her. I tilt her face toward mine and kiss her slowly. Not like before. Now I want to taste her, to feel her body against mine. Her hands travel up my back and wind themselves into my hair. I part her lips with my tongue, and she tastes sweet. Her tongue duels with mine and a groan escapes me. As my hands travel down her body, I know if I don't end this soon, I'm going to fuck her against the door. With a growl, I pull myself away and hold her at arm's length.

"Why did you come here today, Addy?"

Addy's eyes widen. "To see if one of the guys could fix my ice machine at the motel. It's broken, and with all the new guests coming to Kat's wedding, I need it to be working."

"I have a few things to take care of here, and then I'll come down, okay?"

A small smile plays on her lips. "Okay, Jonas. Do you want to stay for dinner with Ben and me?"

I know what she's asking. She's testing me. She needs to know I'm serious, and with her, it's always been about Ben, making sure he's safe and loved.

"What does he like for dessert? I'll bring dessert."

Her smile widens. "He's easy… ice cream. Chocolate ice cream. Is six o'clock okay?"

"I'll be there." I embrace her and breathe in the smell of her. It's a subtle smell of apples and vanilla with something else I can never quite place. *I can't believe I wasted all this time when we could have been together.* I kiss her lightly on the lips and pull away. "See you soon."

Opening the door, I watch as she walks across the compound toward town, as do the brothers in the garage. She has a way of making every man in town look at her ass.

CHAPTER 4

DANE

As I walk across the compound, I see Adelynn Turner leave the garage office, and from the way Jonas is looking at her, I know shit is about to hit the fan with the sheriff. When I get within three feet of Jonas, he glances at me.

"Hey, Prez."

"What the fuck, Jonas? You fucking with the sheriff's woman?" I ask.

Anger flashes across his features. "She doesn't belong to the sheriff. He's never even sealed the deal. Addy and I are going to give it another go."

Fuck. I drop my eyes to my boots. *This is going to be a fucking mess.* "You better be sure, brother, 'cause if we didn't have problems with him before, we will now."

"I'll speak to him, Dane. I'll sort it out."

"Is Dirt here?"

"Yeah, he's in the garage working on an old Chevy. I'll come with."

"You sure about Addy, brother? She has a son, yeah?"

"Yes, I'm sure. I never really got over her the first time. I wasn't sure how to fix it, and yeah, she has a son, Ben."

I say nothing else. If it's one thing I've learned about Jonas over the years, once he's decided about something, it would take an act of God to talk him out of it.

As we get to the working bays of the garage, I hear Dirt yelling, "You mother-fucking-bastard, just fucking go in!" Followed by much laughter from the other brothers within the garage.

"Dirt!" I shout.

He rolls out from under the truck. "Yeah, Prez?" He's covered in grease and grime, with a cigarette hanging out of his mouth.

"Everything okay?"

"Yes, can't get a bolt to go in and stay in, must have stripped the thread."

I grin at him. "The sheriff wants to talk to you. Need you to come up to the clubhouse."

"You can tell that motherfucker I paid my fine!" he growls out as he stands.

"No, Dirt, it's about Kat and the phone call she

received earlier."

He grabs a rag from the back pocket of his overalls then takes a drag of his cigarette. "Give me a second to clean up." He gets up off the ground and heads for the change rooms.

"VP, is Judge here?" I ask.

"Behind you, brother," says Judge.

"You're one quiet fucker when you want to be, aren't you, Judge?" Jonas remarks.

"Sorry, saw the Prez walking across the lot, thought I'd say hello," Judge drawls out with a shit-eating grin on his face.

There are times I'd like to beat Judge senseless, as he's such a cocky fucker, but my woman likes him, and I know he'll always keep her safe. I don't always appreciate the way he looks at her, either, but I know he's not dumb enough to take it further.

"I need you, Jonas, and Dirt to come up to the clubhouse and have a talk with the sheriff."

Dirt appears in front of me in his colors with most of the grease off his face. "Is there a problem, Prez?"

"Gareth Goodman escaped from the psychiatric hospital he was in."

All three of them talk at once.

"Fucking hell!"

"Do they think that fucker is on his way here?"

"Is Kat in danger?"

I hold my hands up. "Let's take it to the

clubhouse and talk to the sheriff. They don't think he'd be stupid enough to come after her, but we'll need to keep a closer eye on her. If he does come here, I want this settled once and for all. I'll *not* have my woman going through this again. So, tell the sheriff what he needs to know, but nothing else. If Goodman turns up in our town, we'll deal with him in our own way."

Everyone agrees, and we make our way toward the clubhouse.

CHAPTER 5

SHERIFF CARLOS MORALES

After the meeting with the Savage Angels members, I walk outside toward my cruiser. As I open the door, Jonas comes up to me.

"Sheriff, can I talk to you?"

"Sure, Jonas, did you want to add anything else?" I take off my hat and toss it onto the passenger seat. He looks like he has something to say by the frown on his face and the way he rubs the back of his neck.

"You and I haven't always seen eye to eye, but you have to know I have a certain amount of respect for you." He places both hands on his hips now and is staring at me, keeping direct eye contact.

"I appreciate that, Jonas, but if you have concerns about Kat and her security, you have to know we'll do everything within our power to protect her."

He shakes his head. "This has nothing to do with Kat. It's about Addy."

And with those three little words, I realize why he's looking so uncomfortable. I slam the door to my cruiser and stand chest to chest with him.

"Addy? Why is Addy any of *your* concern?"

"Sheriff, Carlos, you have to know about us. I know she wouldn't have kept it a secret from you."

"No, she didn't keep it a secret. She told me how you walked out on her without so much as a goodbye, and when you finally came back to town, you didn't so much as wave at her. So, yeah, Jonas, she told me."

I watch as he recoils from my words and closes his eyes. He cusses, and then opens them.

"I fucked it up, but I'm... no, *we* are going to try again."

"*We?*" I whisper.

Anger clouds my vision, and before I realize it, I slam my fist into his face. I hear shouting around me, but my concentration is all on Jonas. His lip is split and bleeding. He advances on me, hits my jaw, and I taste blood. Then he swings again, but I duck and give him an uppercut to his jaw. He stumbles backward, and I tackle him, both of us trading blows as we roll around in the dirt. I get to my feet, and his fist impacts my eye, knocking me down. As he descends on me, I kick out his knee, and he howls in pain as he goes down. This gives me enough time to get to my feet, and as I turn to face him and pummel his face, I feel cold, icy water hit me. The shock of it makes us both stop and turn.

"What the hell do you two think you're doing? Carlos Morales, *you* are the law in this town, and Jonas White, *you* are the vice president of the Savage Angels! What kind of example are you both setting?"

I look at Jonas, who laughs, he's dripping wet like me with blood running down his chin. My laughter rumbles up and out of my chest as we stand looking at Kat Saunders with an empty bucket in her hands and a look of anger on her face.

"This is *not* a laughing matter! You two need to work this out like civilized people! The press is everywhere!"

I look over my shoulder, and sure enough, a group of reporters is behind the gate, snapping away with their cameras. *Fuckers, do they not have anything better to do with their time?* I stare up at the sky, let out a few choice words, and shake my head.

"Sheriff, we good?" Jonas asks.

I drop my head and stare him in the eye. "You hurt her again, and I'll make you wish you'd never been born. Do you get me?" If Addy has gone back to him, there's not a lot I can do.

"I'm not that man anymore, and if I hurt her

again, I'd expect nothing less."

I nod and drop my gaze to the front of my shirt. It's wet, covered in diluted blood and dirt, and the pocket is ripped. *Fucking fantastic.*

"She's a good woman, and she deserves to be happy."

"Yes, she is, Carlos."

At the mention of my name, I look back at him. He's holding out his hand. I take a moment, then grasp it in my own. Kat walks up to us and hands each of us a towel.

"You two okay now?" she asks suspiciously.

"Yes, Kat, but we had it under control," Jonas mutters.

"Yeah, Kat, we did," I agree.

"You had it *under* control? Look at both of you! You could have—"

"Kat, darlin', how about we let them sort this out themselves?" Dane stares at his soon-to-be bride, grabs her by the hand, and walks back inside the clubhouse.

The MC members around us slowly go back to what they were doing, leaving Jonas and me alone.

"Think I'm going to take the rest of the day off. See you around, Jonas."

"Yeah, Carlos, see you around." He gingerly touches his face.

I grin at him and get in my cruiser. In my heart, I knew I'd left it too long with Addy, but she's the only woman in town I can stand to be around. The rest only want a source of income or the prestige of dating the town sheriff. Addy was different. She never kept Jonas a secret from me, but I really thought she had moved on.

As I sit in my cruiser, I pick up the radio and press the button to talk into it. "This is Sheriff Morales, is anyone there?"

"Yes, Sheriff, it's Annie." She's the receptionist at the station.

"Annie, I'm taking the rest of the day off. Be back in tomorrow."

"Is everything all right, Sheriff?"

"Yes, Annie, just taking a personal day. If there's any news on Gareth Goodman, or you think I should know about *anything*, please contact me."

"Yes, sir, of course."

No doubt it will spread like wildfire that I got into it with a member of the Savage Angels MC, but I don't give a fuck. It's been one hell of a day, and I need to go home and drink myself into a stupor.

CHAPTER 6

JONAS

It's five thirty, and I've had ice on my lip for most of the afternoon to get the swelling down. The sheriff surprised me with his reaction. Normally, he's cool, calm, and collected. I never expected him to erupt as he did.

I'm standing in line at the supermarket with ice cream and flowers waiting to checkout. More than a few of the locals look at me and smile. I'm sure the entire town knows we got into it. And I couldn't give a shit. There are many unfamiliar faces in town—the wedding has captured the attention of the nation—hell, the world. Some of the brothers are getting laid regularly by all the new talent in town, hoping to get closer to Kat. We've had to stop newcomers from coming into the compound as it's not safe for her. As I pay for my items, a club angel comes up to me.

"Hey, Jonas, nice lip."

"Hey, Stella, thanks." She's been with the club for years. I think we've all fucked her, but none of us recently.

"You got a date?" she says, licking her lips.

"Something like that."

"Well, if you aren't busy later?" She trails a hand down between her breasts.

"I'll be busy. See you around, Stella." I stride away from her toward the truck, which belongs to the garage.

She's the joke of the compound. She was pretty once, but the life of an unattached Angel can be hard. Stella always made it clear she wanted to be someone's old lady, but no one wants the town whore. I'm pretty sure she's fucked everyone in the Tourmaline chapter and a lot of the guys in neighboring chapters, too.

With a shake of my head, I climb into the truck. My head is full of Addy and how I'm going to fix our relationship, and as I pull the door closed, I'm met with resistance. Looking up, Stella is looking like all kinds of angry. Scrubbing a hand over my face, I sigh, I'm not ready for her bullshit.

"You aren't better than me, Jonas! You've fucked me more than once!"

I look at her face, and it's contorted into a mask

of hurt and anger.

"Stella, I never said I was better than you, and yeah, we have fucked more than once, but not in a really long time. I'm not interested anymore, but that's on me, not you." I'm trying to be gentle with her, but it seems to make her worse.

"Fuck you, Jonas! You can't fuck me and not give a shit about me. I'm worth more than that. I'm a woman of my own making, and I am on the path of self-fulfillment!" She slams the door shut and walks away from me.

The path of self-fulfillment? What the fuck? I watch as she stomps off down the sidewalk toward the compound. Her skirt is a little too short, and her top is so tight it leaves nothing to the imagination. She was never my type, a little too needy and slutty, but I could've treated her better. Although she went from my bed to Dirt's and didn't seem to care. Something I witnessed more than once. I thought she was only a party girl, but maybe I was wrong.

The drive to The Country Inn takes me less than five minutes. As I climb out of the truck, Ben bounds up to me.

"Hey, Jonas! Mom says you're staying for dinner after you fix the ice machine." He's a nice kid, all smiles and full of life.

"Sure am, Ben, wanna help me with it?"

"Really?" His eyes shine with excitement.

"Yeah, I could use the help if you aren't busy?"

His smile grows bigger as his head bobs up and down.

"I have to ask Mom, but I'm sure it will be okay!"

"Lead the way, Ben."

We walk inside the office of The Country Inn together and head toward the back. Addy and her dad have a small apartment back there.

"Mom! Jonas said I can help with the ice machine! Is that okay?"

"If Jonas said you can, then you can." She looks at me with her eyebrows raised in an are-you-sure kind of way.

"It's always good to have an extra pair of hands on a job." I grin at her and hold up the flowers. "These are for you, they aren't as pretty as you, but I remembered you liked yellow daisies."

Something I can't read flashes across her face as she takes them from me. I glance at Ben, who's watching his mother with no small amount of love on his face.

"Thank you, Jonas, they are lovely."

"And this..." I hand Ben a gallon container of chocolate ice cream, "... is for you. But I'm kind of hoping you'll share it with your mother and me."

"Chocolate! My favorite! Of course, I'll share. Thank you, Jonas." His mega-watt smile is contagious.

He rushes out of the room with it. I'm assuming to put it in the freezer. I watch him go, and as I turn back to Addy, she moves into my space and kisses me.

"What was that for?" I wrap my arms around her lower back. She's not getting away from me so easily.

"You remembered. You remembered I loved yellow and daisies. Thank you." Her eyes travel over my face, then lock with mine. "What happened to your face?"

"Carlos and I worked it out."

She tries to pull away from me, but I lock my arms around her tighter. It's my turn to kiss her. Angling my head, I softly press my lips to hers.

Addy lets out the cutest of moans, then her arms slowly move their way up my body until her hands entwine in my hair.

My own hands move to explore what was once mine when I hear a very loud cough from behind me. Addy jumps backward and I reach out to steady her.

"Ben!" Her cheeks flush, and I know she's embarrassed. "You need to show Jonas where the ice machine is, and I'll finish getting dinner ready."

"Come on, Jonas, it's this way." He gives me a goofy grin as he heads toward the front of the Inn.

I look at Addy, who's shaking her head, and I say, "Best go fix your machine."

The ice machine was easy to fix, and Ben has a good head for mechanical problems. He's a smart kid, and made a point of telling me his mom is a good person who deserves to be treated right. In his own way, he told me to mind myself. I respect him for that.

Addy cooked dinner, my favorite, roast chicken and vegetables. It's been a while since someone cared enough to cook what I like. Ben shared his ice cream, and we all watched television in their living room enjoying each other's company. The conversation was fast and easy, and Ben seemed happy to have me in his home with his mom.

I'm sitting on the couch listening to Addy in the next room as she makes sure Ben has done all of his homework before he goes to bed. It can't be easy for her, living here at the Inn with her dad. There's not a lot of privacy for her or Ben. She comes back into the room with a glass of water and hands it to me.

"Sorry, there's no beer. With Dad in the house, I don't keep alcohol around."

"Water is fine," I say to her, but a beer right about now would be good. It's a pleasant way to finish a satisfying meal with good company.

She sits on the couch next to me with one leg tucked up under her.

I smile at her and say, "Come here, Addy."

"I'm right next to you, Jonas."

"Love, you aren't fucking close enough. Come here."

She turns to me and says, "Ben is right next door, and my dad will be home soon."

I push her backward on the couch and lie on top of her. "Then you'll have to be quick and quiet."

"Jonas!" she whispers. "We can't!"

I kiss her as my hand travels to the hem of her skirt. I let my hand slowly trail up the inside of her thigh, and I deepen the kiss, running my tongue along her lips and pushing into her very willing mouth. Lightly, I run my fingers across the flimsy material of her panties, and her breath catches. Sitting up, I throw off my jacket, spread her legs, and push my face up against her panty-clad pussy. She arches, and I suck the material, using my fingers to rub against her clit. A cry escapes her, and I stop.

"Now, love, you need to be quiet, or Ben will hear."

She nods, a sexy smile on her lips. I reach into my back pocket and retrieve my pocket knife. I open it and watch her face as she realizes what I'm about to do. I cut through the material of her panties carefully, then put my knife and her panties in my back pocket. Smirking down at her, I go back to her sweet-smelling cunt.

The taste of her is enough to drive me wild, and my tongue works her as I slip two fingers inside of her. She lifts her hips, arching off the couch, and grinds her pussy into my face. Her movements become more erratic, and a moan escapes her lips. I know she's close.

Abruptly, I stop and sit up. "Addy, where's your bedroom?" I stand and hold out my hand. Need is etched into her face. She slowly places her hand in mine as I help her to her feet, and we make our way to her bedroom.

Once inside, I lock the door, then go to her dresser and look through it. I find a pair of stockings and a scarf.

"Take off your clothes, Addy." She turns her back to me and pulls her shirt over her head. "No, Addy, face me. You have an amazing body, and I want to see it."

She undoes her skirt, and it falls to the ground, then does the same with her bra. I pull my t-shirt over my head as quickly as possible, so I can continue to gaze at her. Then I take off my boots and release my cock from the constricting confines of my jeans. Finally, we're both naked, staring at each other.

I've missed her. The need to fuck her overwhelms me, and if I don't fuck her soon, I'll explode all over her.

Walking up to her, I fold the headscarf in my hand.

"Open your mouth, love."

She does as she's told, and I secure it over her mouth with a knot at the back.

"This will help muffle the noise, so no one hears. Lay on the bed with your arms over your head." Again, she does as she's told, and I straddle her with my cock close to her gagged mouth. I tie her hands to the headboard with the stockings and slowly make my way back down her beautiful body.

I lick her nipple and blow on it, wanting it to stand at attention before I take it into my mouth. She arches her body and strains against her bindings. My hand trails down her body slowly, making its way to her pussy. She's so wet, my fingers easily plunge into her. Slowly, I withdraw them and use my thumb on her sweet spot, increasing my rhythm. The smell of her arousal draws me down between her legs, and I suck on her clit, tasting her. I'd forgotten how good she tastes, smells, and feels. There have been others, but none have ever affected me the way Addy does. Her scent has always been enticing, when I realize it's exclusive to Addy, she smells like home to me, a safe haven.

Someone I could easily claim as mine.
Mine.

Yes, Addy belongs to me.

Her moans, even with the gag on, are becoming louder and more urgent, and I'm glad Ben is asleep. I stop and make my way to her nightstand, opening it as this is where she used to hide the condoms. Thankfully, they're still there. My cock strains as I sheath it in the confining rubber. I kneel on the bed and smile down at her—she's beautiful. Her hair is splayed across the pillows, her nipples are erect, and her eyes are filled with need.

"I'm going to fuck you now, Addy." She shakes her head from side to side. "No?"

A garbled "please" escapes her gagged mouth.

"You want me to finish?" She nods, and I bend down and kiss the inside of her thigh. "Like this?" I lick her pussy and lock my eyes with hers. She nods again, and I continue to feast on her as she places her legs over my shoulders, keeping me in place with her firm thighs. Her movements increase, and I can tell by her taste she's close. She opens up her legs even further, so I increase my speed. Our gazes meet, and she's arched up, looking down at me as her sex clenches. Her moans echo around the room, and even with the gag on, she's less than quiet.

When I'm sure she's finished, I move up her body and place my cock at her entrance and slowly push myself into her. For a moment, I close my eyes, relishing in the feel of her around my cock. The tightness, the feeling of coming home and being with the right woman, she's not only a fuck, but someone I care about. Reaching up, I pull down the gag and kiss her deeply, all the while increasing my speed as I pound in and out of her. She feels amazing, and I can feel my release building with every thrust. My hands find her bound wrists, and our fingers link. I'm worried I'm crushing her, but she's moving her hips in rhythm with mine, and I can feel as she clenches and unclenches her core. Her ability to do this has always been a huge turn-on for me. I thrust into her one last time and feel her constrict around my cock, sending me over the edge. The wave of pleasure washes over me, through me, and as it always is with Addy, I feel whole, complete, sated. There's a line of sweat across her top lip, and tears run quietly down her face.

"Love, what's wrong?" She shakes her head and tries to bury her face into the pillow. I release her from her bindings and pull her up onto my chest, stroking her back. "Did I hurt you?" I whisper.

"No. I'm just..." Her tears flow more freely, and I hold her tighter.

"Do you want me to go?" I ask.

She grips me more firmly for a moment, then sits up and stares me in the eyes. "That's the problem, Jonas, I don't want you to leave, ever again."

"I promise you, love, no, I fucking swear it on my colors, I'm *never* leaving you again." I wipe her tears away and then ask, "So, do you like the left or right side of the bed?"

"What?" Her eyebrows have come together, and she looks confused.

"To sleep on, the right or left?"

"Jonas, you can't—"

"Addy, I meant it when I said I wanted to make this work, and love, this is me, making it work." I'm surprised at my own words, but I mean what I say, and I don't want to go back to an empty bed at the compound, alone.

"Jonas, there are Ben and my father. I have to consider them."

"Love, you're a grown woman, and your father needs to realize you have a life of your own. Ben will bounce off you. If you're okay with this, he'll be okay with this."

"I'm not sure…"

"I'm staying tonight, and in the morning, we'll look at getting a place of our own. Somewhere in town, so you can be close to the motel, and I can be close to the club."

She sits up and moves away from me. I know she's confused, and I know she wants this, but I also know I have a lot to make up for.

"Love, you can pick the—"

"Okay."

"Okay?" I question.

"Yes, Jonas, okay. We're going to do this, and you

better keep your promises to me 'cause, honey, if you fuck me over on this, you won't get another chance."

Her words take me by surprise. Laughter rumbles up out of my chest, and I grab her, pulling her onto my lap.

"If I fuck you over?" I chuckle. "No, love, I'll *not* fuck you over."

She's smiling and bites the side of her bottom lip. Her hair is a mess, and she looks sexy as hell.

"Good." She repositions herself, so she's straddling me and kisses me deeply. Her hands go from my chest and weave themselves into my hair. "Let's shower, and you can seal this deal with more lovemaking."

I roll, so I'm on top of her. "Addy, I don't make love, I fuck, but I do love fucking you."

"Okay, let's seal this deal with a fuck." She winks.

"I'm not sure if I like you using all this foul language. It's not fucking like you."

"People change, I've changed," she says.

"Love, you haven't changed that fucking much. Now, get your ass into the shower so that I can seal this deal."

I roll off her and watch her sexy ass move as she makes her way into the bathroom. My cock hardens as I stare at her, knowing from this moment on, Addy and I are a team.

CHAPTER 7

SHERIFF CARLOS MORALES

It's been two days since my run-in with Jonas. He and Addy seem to be moving at a ridiculous speed—they've gone from not speaking to each other to moving in together. The entire town is talking about our fight, and now, they are looking at houses together. I'm glad he finally made his mind up. I just wish it had been about another woman.

Now, I'm standing outside where Bruce's Bakery was. Ash and dirt cover the ground as I wait for the Fire Marshall to give me his expert opinion on what happened.

"Sheriff, how do you think this happened?" Bruce, the owner, asks.

"I'm assuming you left your ovens on? Something caught on fire?" I reply.

"Sheriff, I've been doing this for over thirty years, and I've never had a fire." Shock and disbelief are etched onto his features as if my questions were a personal affront.

"You saying you think this was deliberate?"

He shuffles from foot to foot and looks at his boots. "I'm saying my insurance is barely going to cover my costs, and if I were going to have a fire, I'd have insured it for more."

"How about we wait to hear what the Fire Marshall says?"

He nods his head and looks up at the approaching man.

"Sheriff, do you want to hear my findings, or do we need to go somewhere more private?" the Fire Marshal asks.

"Here is fine. Bruce, here, didn't do it." I fold my arms across my chest and point in Bruce's direction.

"How do you know?"

"I know 'cause I've been doing this a long time," I say, slightly annoyed at the Fire Marshall.

"The fire was set intentionally. It started by the backdoor where I found the remains of a fuel can." He holds up an evidence bag. "They weren't too smart. If it had been started around or near one of the ovens, we might have thought it was an accident, but they didn't even try hard to conceal it. Even a novice could tell it was done on purpose."

I glance at Bruce, whose face has gone a shade of red, and his lips are drawn into a thin line. "Bruce, you know of any reason someone would do this? You got any enemies?"

"No, Sheriff. I have no idea why anyone would do this. But *you* know there are a lot of strangers in town."

I look back at the Fire Marshall. "When will you have the official report to me?"

"Later today, I'll give you the preliminary, end of the week for the complete report."

He walks away, and I turn to Bruce. "Could you come down to the station to fill in some reports? We can contact your insurance company at the same time." He agrees and walks with me to the sidewalk. "Bruce, do you want a lift?"

"No thanks, Sheriff. I need time to think, and the short walk to your station will do me good."

He wanders off down Main Street, and as I watch him go, I can see the town's mayor walking toward me.

"Hello, Sheriff. Did Bruce leave his ovens on?"

"No Justice, this was arson." We stare at the ashes of the burned-out bakery.

He raises his eyebrows at me and lets out a whistle. "Any ideas on who did it?"

"Not yet, but we'll find out."

"Well, have a good day, Sheriff. If I can be of any help, you know where to find me."

"Thanks, Justice. See you tonight at the meeting?"

"Yes, but I swear this wedding is going to be the death of me. It might be good for the economy, but I'll be happy when everything goes back to normal, and Kat Saunders and her entourage leave."

I chuckle at him. "See you tonight."

Shaking hands, we head in separate directions, me toward my cruiser and Justice to Betty's Café.

Walking to my cruiser, I silently agree with him. When the wedding is over and done with, I hope my town will go back to the way it was.

CHAPTER 8

KAT

It's a beautiful day in Tourmaline. The sun is shining, and I'm in my Mustang heading for the Savage Angels' compound. My security detail now comprises six members of the MC. I think Dane would be happier if I stayed home until the wedding was over, but I still have a few more things to organize, and I want to do as much of the wedding planning as I can. The brothers ride three in front and three in back, making sure I can't speed.

What's the point of having a Mustang if I can't use it to its best potential?

Inwardly, I sigh as I pull in and park at the compound.

Judge opens my door and helps me to my feet.

"You'd make a good valet."

"I've already got a job, sugar."

"I'm just saying."

"What's the plan for today?"

"I thought I'd walk into town, and…"

Before I can finish, Judge shakes his head at me. "No can do, sugar. You'll either be on the back of a bike or preferably in your car, but no walking. Too many strangers in town, and it's too hard to protect you."

This time I let out a sigh anyone within five feet could hear. "Fine, I'll *drive* into town and go see Bruce at the bakery…" He's shaking his head at me again. "Why can't I go see Bruce? Jesus, Judge, he's making my wedding cake for fuck's sake!" I raise my voice, and more than a few of the brothers have stopped to listen in on our conversation.

Judge has one hand on his hip, the other one is held palm up in front of me, and he's smirking as he says, "Sugar, it's not that you *can't* go see Bruce, you *can*, but his bakery burned down last night."

All the pent-up anger leaves me as I stand there and shake my head at him. "How? Is Bruce okay?"

"He's fine. He wasn't there when it happened. Probably left the ovens on or something. Rumor has it he's at the sheriff's office. Who knows, maybe he did it himself."

Judge gently grabs my elbow and guides me into the clubhouse. Standing at the bar is Kade, and, as usual, Zeke and JJ surround him. They all look at me as I head toward Dane's room.

"He's not in there," says Kade.

I stop and stare at him. It's not that I don't like Kade, but he scares me a little. He's kind of intense, and there are times when he seems downright hostile toward me.

"Where's the Prez, then?" Judge questions.

He flicks his gaze from me to Judge. "He's in the garage. One local asked if he'd personally work on his car. It's been a while since he's pulled spanners, so he said yes." His gaze comes back to me. "I could walk you over if you'd like?"

Judge intervenes before I can respond. "Kat is *my* responsibility. If she's going anywhere, it will be with *me*."

The atmosphere in the bar has gone frosty. Zeke and JJ straighten up, and I can tell this is about to turn hostile, so I do the only thing I can think of, I laugh.

"Okay, okay, there's enough male testosterone in the air to last me a lifetime!" I say, as I try to get myself under control. "I'm perfectly capable of taking myself across the compound to find my man. Feel free to duke it out while I'm gone."

I turn on my heel and stalk across the lot toward Dane, all the while thinking about the fact my wedding cake is now not going to happen. As I enter the garage, I see him in overalls laughing with one of the brothers, grease smeared across his face, and when he looks at me, I burst into tears. In seconds, he's across the room and has me in his arms, wrapped in his hulking frame.

"Darlin', what's wrong? Did that fucker, Gareth, call you again?" His arms tighten around me.

"N-no," I sputter out. "The bakery burned down, and we won't have a wedding cake."

He seems relieved by his exhale, the tension I feel in his body evaporates, and he whispers, "Thank God, that's all it is."

"That's *all* it is?" I shriek at him. "That's *all*!"

"Darlin', it's not the end of the world. We'll get another cake made."

"Oh, really? And how will we do it with less than two weeks before the wedding?"

"What's the stupid catch-phrase Dave is always saying?" Dave is the manager of my band, The Grinders.

"He says public perception is everything, and he can spin anything, but this *isn't* a PR problem. How can he help?"

"I have a feeling Dave would move heaven and earth to make sure you're happy. Let's go into the office and call him." He turns me around and ushers me toward the office. "And darlin', he isn't the only one."

When we enter the office, he locks the door and closes the blinds.

"What are you doing?" I ask.

"Giving us some privacy."

"Dane, why do we need privacy to call Dave?"

"You're wearing a skirt, a short skirt, and I want to fuck you over the desk." I walk backward, and he prowls toward me with a knowing smile across his handsome face. "Darlin', there's nowhere to run, and it's been far too long since you and I have had sex. I can't wait till the wedding. If you wanted me to wait, you should *not* have worn a fucking short skirt." He unbuttons his jeans and I lick my lips. I need to focus.

"Dane! It's just over a week until the wedding—"

"It's closer to two weeks, and I want you."

My ass is against the desk, and when he reaches me, he lifts me onto it and spreads my legs. His mouth descends on mine, and his hands are everywhere. A moan escapes me before I can protest. We had agreed to wait, to make the wedding night special, but all my objections fall away as my body responds to him.

"I like you in skirts," he murmurs as his hands hook my panties and pulls them down. "I like the easy access."

My hands have a mind of their own, and I find myself pulling open his overalls. The muscles of his chest feel fantastic and stretch the material of his t-shirt as I explore his well-defined body. He steps back from me, grabs me around the waist, and places me on my feet, where he turns me around. He pushes me, so I'm bent over the desk, and I scatter the top of it onto the floor. I hear him unzip his jeans, and then I feel him at my entrance as he aggressively pushes his way inside me. I gasp at the first thrust as he grips my hips and moves in and out of me at a pounding speed.

He twists my hair in his fist, making me arch backward, and growls, "Tell me you've missed me, tell me you fucking want this as much as I fucking do."

"I've missed you, baby," I say breathlessly.

His thrusts increase and become more forceful, and the harder he fucks me, the hotter I feel. I'm sure I am about to melt when he buries himself inside me and lets out a grunt of satisfaction. I can hear his heavy breathing, but I'm not finished. I try to move my hips, but he pulls my hair harder, forcing me to stop. When his breathing calms down, he pulls out of me and lets go of my hair. My body is crying for a release, and I feel him move away from me. Frustration washes through me as I stand and turn to face him.

"I haven't finished."

"You didn't tell me you wanted it as much as I did. Do you?"

"Yes," I hiss at him. "I want it as much as you do!"

An arrogant smirk crosses his features. "So, you

want me to finish?"

"Yes, I want you to finish!"

"Get your ass up onto the desk, darlin', and lay back."

I do as I'm told and hold his gaze as he trails his fingers up my thighs. When he reaches my pussy, he plunges his fingers inside of me, and his thumb works my sweet spot. The burn inside of me increases as I grind into his hand. My orgasm builds and builds until it washes over me, and I cry out his name. His hand continues to fuck me until I've had enough. When he stops, I open my eyes, and he's smiling down at me.

"You look beautiful. Fucking sexy as hell."

"That felt good. I needed it. Weddings are stressful."

Laughter rumbles up and out of his chest. "It's a great stress-reliever. Now, let's get cleaned up and phone Dave."

CHAPTER 9

DAVE LAWRENCE
PR Manager

I'm listening to Dark Ink as they polish the last track on their new album. The tension between Dan and Amy is again flaring toward a volcanic eruption as they bicker back and forth over a guitar riff. It reminds me of Truth and Jasmin from The Grinders. Thankfully, they never slept together, but I have it on good authority, Dan and Amy have been going hard at it for the last month. I'm about to intervene when my phone buzzes. Grabbing it out of my pocket, I look at the caller ID.

"Well, hello, princess!"

"Hey, Dave, how are you?" Kat's beautiful voice greets me, and I can hear something isn't right. She's not her usual bubbly self.

"What's wrong?" I've been her manager for a long time, and I think of her as the daughter I never had. Silence fills the line. "Kat, are you okay?"

I hear her sniffle. "Th-the bakery burned down."

"The bakery burned down?" I'm confused. "What does it have to do with you?"

"They were making my wedding cake." I can hear more sniffles and some kind of noise on the other end of the line.

"Dave? It's Dane. Our girl is upset, and I told her you could fix this. Can you?"

"Of course, I can fix it. Why is she so upset? Our girl doesn't normally rattle so quickly." I like Dane, and over the years, he's proven himself to be worthy of my girl, even if he's the president of an MC. I can hear muffled voices as Kat says something to him.

"Dave, can you come to Tourmaline earlier than next week? Is it possible?"

"Of course I can. Is she all right?"

"Gareth Goodman escaped from the hospital and rang Kat. They don't think he'll come here, but I think she'd appreciate having family around her right now."

"Why didn't she ring me when she found out he'd escaped? And why haven't I heard about this on the fucking news?" I demand, anger coloring my tone.

"I have no idea why it isn't in the news, and Kat didn't want to worry you."

"Kat didn't want to worry me? Jesus, Mary, and the twelve apostles! You just called me family! Family gets told about this, this... shit!"

He chuckles into the phone. "This shit? Dave, man, it was her call, and she worries about you. How soon can you get here?"

"I'll leave today, and I'll bring everyone with me. You have room, I assume?"

"Yeah, man, *we* have room."

"See you soon." I hang up without waiting for a response.

I look into the recording booth in time to see Dan scrunch up the music sheets and throw them at Amy. The rest of the band is laughing and smirking as they go at each other. Again. I have more important issues to worry about and don't have time for this.

I flip a switch so I can be heard in the booth. "Enough!" I roar at them. All members of Dark Ink stop and look at me. "Pack up your shit, we're done for today, and you can pack your bags, too."

They recoil at my words and have their mouths open.

Dan is the first to speak, "Dave, it's part of our process. You know we don't mean it. Come on, man, telling us to pack up is one thing, but our gear, too?"

I realize what I've said. They think I mean to fire them. A small smile plays on my lips. "Dan, my boy, you're under contract with me for a good long while. I have no intention of letting you out of it over a spat with Amy. We're all going to Tourmaline, so you can finish this last fucking song there." I pause and take them all in. They're young, but they need to learn to get along if they want a long career in this industry. "On the road to Tourmaline, I expect you *all* to sit down as a band and sort this shit out."

As a group, they all agree. Dan looks at Amy, who sighs and puts her drumsticks down.

"Dave?" Amy asks questioningly.

"Yes, Amy?"

"Are The Grinders going to be there?" Dan's head turns so quickly, I think it will snap off. He reaches for his jacket and storms out of the booth, slamming the door as he leaves.

"Yes, Amy, they'll be there. May I suggest you sort out your problem with Dan *before* you see any of them? It would be a shame to have to find a new drummer."

Her mouth hangs open as I stand and make my way out of the recording studio. I have no intention of dropping her from the band, but she's the one to cause this tension between her and Dan. The last time she saw Truth from The Grinders, they had a month-long affair. It's been a couple of years since she's seen him, but asking if they'll be there only served to upset Dan. Hopefully, they can sort this out themselves, or someone will have to go.

I stalk out of the building into the sunshine, and a few moments later, my limousine arrives. I dial one of my assistants once I'm settled inside.

"Hello, Mr. Lawrence."

"Greetings, Veronica."

"How may I help you today?" she asks pleasantly.

"I need you to organize for The Grinders, Dark Ink, and myself to be in Tourmaline ASAP."

"I thought Dark Ink needed to finish their album?" I can hear the clicking of a keyboard as she speaks.

"They will, in Tourmaline, at Kat's studio."

"Yes, sir."

"Oh, and Veronica, I want Dark Ink to go by bus. They have shit to sort out, and I'll need you to accompany them. Is that a problem?"

"No, sir. I can do it."

"Good. I also need a wedding cake organized for Kat. Seems she's having an issue."

"Done. Anything else?" Veronica is one of my favorite assistants. Nothing is ever too much trouble, and she's efficient.

"Yes, find out all you can about Gareth Goodman. Who has visited him? Who has phoned him? Everything for the last two years."

"I'm on it."

"Thank you, Veronica, and for the love of God, please call me Dave."

"Yes, sir, I'll work on it."

I click off and smirk at the phone. She's worked for me for years and does everything I ask, except call me Dave.

CHAPTER 10

ADELYNN

The atmosphere in Tourmaline feels more electric the closer we get to Kat and Dane's wedding. The Inn is fully booked, and I've had to employ another girl to help me keep the rooms clean and tidy. My father is playing the well-behaved innkeeper and managing very well. He's even accepted Jonas into our lives.

I'm standing at the reception desk when in walks a heavily pregnant Emily Agostino.

"Adelynn! How are you?"

"Oh my God, Emily! Look at you!" I rush around the counter and into her arms. Emily is Dane's sister and one of my closest friends. Her help getting my father into an AA program was a lifeline.

"I know, *look* at me!" She points to her

burgeoning belly.

"Amare, you look beautiful."

I pull away to see Salvatore, her husband, standing in the doorway with their baby boy, Vincent, in his arms.

"I do *not*! I look like a whale!" She pulls out of my arms and walks to him, putting her arms around them both.

He shakes his head at her, looks at me, and says, "Tell her, Adelynn, tell her how beautiful she is."

"Sal is right, Emily, you look beautiful." Emily shakes her head at me. "How long do you have?"

"Four *endless weeks*!" She laughs at me.

Vincent holds out his hands to me, and I walk over and take him out of Sal's arms. "You're getting huge, little man!" I tickle him, and he giggles and squirms in my arms.

Sal claps his hands and holds them out to his son, who instantly tries to get out of my arms and back into his father's.

"Emily insisted on stopping here to say hello before we go out to the main house. I'm going to take Vincent to Bettie's, so you two can catch up. I'll be leaving Tony with you in case you need anything."

Sal is part of the Abruzzi crime family, and Tony is his right-hand man. There's no one he trusts more with his family. He grabs his wife by the neck and kisses her lips before kissing her forehead.

"I won't be long," says Emily.

"Take your time, amare." He flashes me his grin, which would make any girl wish he were single, but one look at him with Emily, and you can see he's totally in love with her.

I watch her face as she watches them both go, a look of devotion plastered across her face. Slowly, she turns to me and says, "I need to get off my feet. My back is killing me." Panic crosses her features. "Please don't tell Sal, he worries, and I don't need him to be any more protective than he already is."

"Your secret is safe with me," I say, holding up one hand and the other to my chest.

She laughs and says, "Lead me to your couch."

We're sitting at the kitchen table, catching up when Emily asks, "Okay, spill, tell me *what* or *who* has you so happy?"

I let out a nervous laugh. "What do you mean?"

"Come on, Addy, we've been friends long enough for me to see you're positively glowing! Has Carlos finally made his move?"

"No, it's not Carlos. It is Jonas."

Concern flashes across her face. "Jonas? Jonas,

who left you and didn't say why? Jonas, who you told me you were done with? *That* Jonas?"

"Yes, Emily, that Jonas," I say sternly.

"Hey, don't get me wrong, I *like* Jonas. He's been nothing but nice to me, especially with my incident here in town, but from what *you* have told me, he didn't exactly treat you very well."

Emily went missing in Tourmaline a couple of years ago. I know Jonas was instrumental in finding her, and I always thought there was more to it, but everyone stuck to the story, she wandered off and got lost.

"He's changed, Em. He's so different, it's scary."

"Scary good or scary bad?"

"Scary good."

She slaps my arm and laughs. "That's the best kind! I want to hear *all* the details! Leave nothing out. After all, I'm a boring, married, pregnant woman. I need to live vicariously through you."

"In fact, we're moving in together next week."

"Shut up! Really? I'm so happy for you!"

I nod and smile at her when Jonas walks through the door.

"Jonas!" I watch as Emily awkwardly gets to her feet.

"Em! Fuck me. How long have you got before you have another rug rat?"

"Four weeks and counting!" She beams up at him.

"Well, I'll give it to Agostino, two kids and a wedding... he keeps it interesting."

"More like he keeps me barefoot and pregnant." She puts both hands on her lower back and stretches it out. "This is the last one for a little while. I need a break."

"You look good, Em. Happy."

"I am, and I hear you and Addy are an item?" She makes it a question as though she wants to hear his side of our relationship.

He grabs my hand and pulls me up off the couch, putting an arm around my waist. "Yes, Addy and I are together."

The grin on Emily's face grows. "Good, but you know you aren't good enough for her, don't you?"

He grins back at her. "Is that fucking right?"

"Yes, it is. She's my best friend. You hurt her, and I'll get Dane to demote you or Sal to make it right."

"Emily, I can't believe you just said that!" I say to her as she giggles and sits back down.

"Oh, Addy, Jonas knows what I mean. Don't you, honey?"

"Love, she's only looking out for you. Can't blame a woman for that." He smirks.

I watch as something flashes across Emily's face, and I drop to my knees in front of her. "Em, are you okay?"

"Oh my God, you're worse than Salvatore! Yes, I'm all right. I'm just tired. Can you get Tony for me?

I think I need to lie down and have a nap."

"I'll go. It's been a while since I've seen that ball of muscle," Jonas says as he heads for the door.

"Well, if I hadn't seen it myself, I'd never have believed it." Emily gestures toward Jonas as he leaves the room.

"Believed what?" I ask.

"The man is taken! The way he looks at you, he's completely smitten. I'm so happy for you, Addy. You deserve a piece of happiness."

"A piece of happiness, where did that come from?" I ask.

"If I could but share with you a piece of happiness, so you would know true contentment, even fleetingly, for the rest of your days, I'd give you some of mine."

"That's beautiful, Em."

"My dad used to say it. I don't know whose quote it is, but it sticks with me, you know?"

I'm nodding as Tony walks through the door.

He envelopes me in a hug and says to Em, "You ready to go, sweetheart?"

"Yes, I am. Time to go see big brother." He lets me go and helps Emily to her feet. When Emily is standing, she moves to me and wraps her arms around me. "You'll come out to the house with Jonas and Ben tomorrow night for dinner?"

"I'd love that."

"Good. I'll get Sal to cook a big Italian dinner for

all of us. It's why I'm so fat... it is all his good cooking."

I burst out laughing. "Em, you aren't fat, honey, you're pregnant!"

"Do *not* remind me!" She chuckles as Tony holds her arm and guides her toward the door.

CHAPTER 11

KAT

Our home is bursting with people. My band, The Grinders, turned up with Dave, and yesterday, Emily, Salvatore, and Vincent arrived. Tonight, we're having dinner, and everyone is invited. Thankfully, Salvatore is cooking, and Emily says he's good. He's certainly good at bossing everyone around in the kitchen. He has both ovens going as well as the pizza oven out on the deck.

It's nice to watch him as he fusses over Emily. He tries to anticipate her every whim before she asks for it and delivers it to her with a smile and a kiss.

If I weren't totally in love with Dane, his smile could sway me in his direction. The man is gorgeous, not as handsome as my Dane, but he does have it.

As if reading my thoughts, I feel Dane's arms circle around me and pull me into his hulking frame. "You all right, darlin'?" He kisses my neck.

"Yes, babe, I'm good. Does everyone have a room?"

He whispers into my ear, "Yes, want to go find one?"

I twist around in his arms. "Not long now, babe."

His blue eyes flash with the promise of sex and intimacy. "We could slip away. There are enough people in our home they probably wouldn't notice or care."

"I want our wedding night to be special, something to remember. Don't you want that, too?"

"Darlin', every time with you is something-fucking-special. Our wedding night will be no different." He kisses me on the lips and pulls me closer. The smell of him and being wrapped up in his arms is almost enough for me to give in.

"My beautiful bride, perhaps you two should get a room?" Truth says loudly.

I pull away from Dane and turn around—the entire room is watching us.

Dane chuckles. "Sounds fucking good to me."

I frown up at him and bat his arms away. "We'll have the rest of our lives for that. Now, Sal, do you need any help?"

"No." He smirks and looks at Truth. "The beautiful bride will not be helping in the kitchen unless, of course, she doesn't mind finding me a good bottle of red?"

"For cooking or drinking?" I ask Sal.

"Does it really matter?" He winks.

"Hell, yes, it does! I'm not giving you a superb bottle of red to cook with!" Exasperation fills my voice.

"Ahh, now there's your first mistake. You should never cook with something which *isn't* good enough to drink."

"*Whatever*, I'll go find you one downstairs in the cellar."

"I'll come with you, princess." I look up as Dave gestures for me to lead the way. He's been trying, unsuccessfully, to get me alone since he arrived. "Your taste in wine typically ends with, is it sweet? And I think Sal will want something with a little more body than that."

Sal chuckles while I roll my eyes as I leave the room.

When we get downstairs, I point at the bottles and say, "Okay, Dave, pick one."

He walks up to them and starts turning bottles over, looking at the labels. "Are we going to have a conversation about your wedding and Gareth?"

"I'm sorry I didn't tell you about Gareth straight away. There's been so much going on it slipped my mind." I try to smile at Dave, but I'm sure it looks fake. "When the bakery burned down, I kind of lost it. That's when we called. I wasn't keeping Gareth from you, but so much more was happening. I felt a little overwhelmed."

"So much more? And the 'so much more' was the bakery burning down? I'll forgive my princess only because I'm sure this wedding has fried your brain."

I slowly draw in a breath and pin Dave with a look of anger. "The wedding has fried my brain? Are you serious?"

"Kat, so far, everything has gone to plan for you. The only thing that's not is your wedding cake, and I have three designs on my phone for you to look at. As for Gareth, I've made inquiries. Did you know he had a photo montage of you on his wall at the hospital?" Before I can respond, he goes on. "I love you like a daughter, Kat, and I worry about you more than you realize."

I wrap my arms around him, and he squeezes me tight. "I love you, too, Dave. I'm truly sorry about the Gareth thing. You don't need to worry about me. Dane has increased my security, and the sheriff has extra men. I'm safe, I promise."

I feel him let out a sigh. "All right, let's choose a red and go look at the cakes I think you'll like. Then you can show me your wedding dress, and I'll show you the suit I got from Armani's to give you away in. It's fabulous."

I look up at him, and his eyes are sparkling. He

has always had good taste in clothes. "Can't wait to see it! My dress is fabulous, too. We're going to steal the show, baby!"

"Oh, princess, we both know all eyes will be on you and your hunky man. I must admit, I'm looking forward to seeing him in a suit." He raises his eyebrows up and down suggestively. Giggling, I slap his arm playfully.

"Dave! Keep your illicit thoughts about my man to yourself!"

"Oh, you're no fun, princess! Now, a bottle of red. I like the look of this 2005 Penfolds Cabernet Sauvignon." He keeps his arm around my shoulders as he guides me back to the stairs. "Are you still happy, princess?"

"Yes, I am. How about you? Did you bring a plus one for the wedding?"

"I haven't invited anyone yet," Dave says as he frowns and looks around, avoiding my gaze.

"I thought you were seeing someone. That guy from Hawaii, Luther?"

He pulls away from me. "That's the problem, he lives in Hawaii, and I live in LA, and neither of us wants to move."

"Dave, you could do what you do from anywhere, and you know it. Time for you to be happy, old man."

He slaps my ass. "Old? Darling, I'm *many* things, but I'll *never* be old!"

We make our way upstairs, laughing at each other. When we enter the kitchen, Dave hands the bottle of red over to Sal, who promptly opens it. I look at Sal questioningly.

"We have to let it breathe, Kat, for a minute. Thank you for getting it for me."

"You're more than welcome. Where is everybody?" I ask.

"Emily went to put Vincent down, Tony went with her," replies Sal, who only notices his own family.

"And everyone else?" I prompt.

He shrugs and points to the back deck. "Perhaps they went outside?" Sal has eyes for one person and one person only, and that's Emily.

"How is dinner coming along?" asks Dave.

"Another half an hour. I need to put the cheesy garlic pizzas in the oven, and then we're good to go."

I shake my head and go in search of Dane. He's on the back deck talking in quiet tones to Judge, who looks worried. As I approach, they stop talking, and Dane pulls me into his side.

"Hey, darlin', we were just talking about you."

"Only good things, sugar, I swear," Judge says with a wink and a wicked grin.

"You both look serious. What's up?" I question.

Dane looks at Judge, who nods slightly, lets out a sigh, and says, "The fire at the bakery was deliberately set. From what we can gather from our source at the sheriff's office, it wasn't done as an insurance scam, so Bruce is in the clear. It has been suggested by some that it was an attack against you." I pull away from Dane and stare at Judge.

"Before you get excited, darlin', we have no proof to support that. What we have is a town overrun with newcomers, and it could also be some sick fucker who likes fires. We know nothing yet, so don't panic, okay?"

"Who thinks it's an attack against me? Where did they get the information from?"

"According to Bruce, he received a call earlier on the day of the fire asking if he was making your wedding cake. He thought it was from a magazine doing a story and thought it would be good for business, so he said yes, but at the end, the caller said, *'we shall see about that'* and promptly hung up. Now, it could be something, or it could be nothing," says Judge, flicking his gaze between us.

"But you think it's something, don't you, Judge?" I question.

"Now, darlin', we don't *know* anything. Could be some fucker is trying to make a point. Whatever the reason is, we don't know. Judge and I think you need to keep a low profile between now and the wedding. Get the fucking wedding planner to do some work." I frown at Dane. "Please, darlin', do it for me?"

Concern is etched into his features, and Judge is nodding in agreement. "Now that Dave is here, I can pull back. He knows my tastes, and he'll be able to make decisions for me. I'm sure between him and the wedding planner, everything will run smoothly."

Relief washes over both their faces as they exchange glances.

"Princess, you must try this bottle of red, it's delicious!" yells Dave from the back door.

"Which one did you get?" asks Dane.

"It's a Penfolds cab sav. It's very good," Dave responds with a grin.

"The 2005 cab sav? From *my* cellar downstairs?"

"Yes, yes, now come have some!"

I grab Dane's hand and pull him toward the house. "Darlin', I was saving that for a special occasion. It is, *was*, a very expensive bottle of red."

"Does it matter? Really? You prefer beer anyway." He looks down at me with no small amount of displeasure, so I grab his face and kiss it. "Come on, big guy, let's go try it."

When we enter the kitchen, it's full of brothers, my band, and everyone else. Sal holds out a glass of red to Dane, who accepts it, and takes a large sip.

"How does it taste?" I ask.

He leans down to my ear. "You're right, I prefer beer."

Laugher bubbles up out of me, and I kiss his

handsome face. "I'll go get you one."

The rest of the evening went well. Sal is an amazing cook and makes the best Spaghetti Bolognese I've ever tasted. He refused to give me the recipe, saying it's a family secret. I told him I was family, and for a moment, he looked conflicted until Emily said she'd give it to me, then he told me, "Of course, I could have it." The way he looks at Emily makes my heart sing, and I was feeling jealous until I glanced at Dane and he had the very same look on his face as he stared at me.

Those of us who are left after dinner are lazing in the family room having coffee and chatting. I watch as Dave wanders in and sits down beside me. He pulls his phone out from his jacket pocket, pushes some buttons, and hands it to me. Looking down at the screen, I see a picture of an enormous wedding cake.

"That's gorgeous!"

"That's the first one. Check out the next two."

As I flick between the pictures, Dane leans in and kisses my forehead. "Which one do you like, darlin'?"

"Which one do *you* like?" I counter.

"Darlin', it's a cake. Unless you're popping out of it, this is your department. Pick whichever one you would like."

"Well, this one has pretty icing flowers down one side, and the way the icing drapes around them is beautiful."

"Okay, that one it is—" says Dane, but I cut him off.

"Well, I didn't say that. This one has pearls and diamantes all over it and would match my dress."

I glance up at Dane, who's looking at me with a look of amusement. "So, this one, then?"

"No, I think it has to be this one… it suits both of us. It's simple for you but has flowers and some bling on it for me." I look at Dave. "Could they make the flowers on top a light pink? But leave everything else as is?"

"Princess, they can do whatever you'd like. I'll send it through now." He pats my leg, grabs his phone, and leaves the room.

Dane plays with my hair, and as I look around the room, I feel a sense of home, love, and family. Truth is sitting talking to Blair, with Jasmin tucked into his side. Jonas, Addy, and Ben are talking to Jamie from The Grinders and he's promising to show Ben how to play the drums. There are more brothers out on the deck. The entire house is full of those I love, and I sigh in contentment.

"You all right, darlin'?"

"Yeah, baby, I'm better than all right. I'm tired, though."

Dane untangles himself from me and stands. "Well, ladies and gents, time for us to hit the hay. Have a good night. Those who are staying, stay, those who aren't, ride safe."

He holds out his hand to me and helps me to my feet.

"Night all, see you tomorrow," I say.

We walk hand in hand to our room. When we enter, I sit on the bed, and Dane kneels before me and removes my shoes. "You going to have a shower, darlin'?"

"Yeah, even though I'm tired, I want one."

"Okay. I need to go back downstairs and see Judge, but I'll be right back."

He stands, kisses the top of my head, and leaves the room.

CHAPTER 12

DANE

I walk downstairs to a waiting Judge.

He smirks at me as I hit the bottom stair. "Thought you might be a little longer, Prez."

"She's tired, and not that it's any of your fucking business, but we're waiting until the wedding night." He raises an eyebrow at me. "No, it's not my fucking idea, but it's what she wants, and I'm all about keeping her happy."

"Speaking of keeping her happy, what would you have done if she'd pushed back on keeping out of town?"

"We both know I'd have made her stay here no matter what. Thank fuck, she didn't argue." I rub a hand over my face. "How many fucking crazies are there in town now, do you think?"

"Too many to count, Prez. I'm going to go back over to the church and Town Hall to make sure security is tight. The only problem is, it's a long time between now and the big fucking day. Anyone or anything *could* get inside."

I'm about to answer when Jasmin comes into the hallway. She walks right up to Judge and throws her arms around him. "Well, well, well, now, baby, I thought you'd left!"

The grin on Judge's face grows. "Now, sugar, do you really think I'd have left *you* without saying goodbye?"

Their on-again-off-again love affair has been going on for as long as I've known Kat. I don't think they are exclusive, but when either is with the other, there's no denying the lust in the air. Both are terrible flirts, and both don't mind casual sex, but when they are together, they work.

I clear my throat, and both turn to look at me.

"We done, Prez?" asks Judge.

"Yeah, brother. I need you to go over the things we talked about, *every day*, twice a day, until the wedding."

"Yes, Prez, I can do it. You have a good night."

He turns his attention back to Jasmin, and I go back upstairs to Kat. It's not easy having a relationship with a famous rock star. It comes with more baggage than I care to think about. When the wedding is over, I hope life and everything will go back to some kind of fucking normalcy. She'll always be in the public eye, and it makes some of my business endeavors harder to manage.

I own strip clubs, brothels, bars, and garages—all of them legit. I'm even expanding into some real estate with Sal. He's slowly moving away from the Abruzzi crime family, and I'm slowly pulling my club away from drugs, guns, and anything else which could get us locked up.

We never run anything illegal out of Tourmaline. Well, we never used to. One of my men, Fith, started running guns. He had quite a nice business going, and we've been searching for the one point five million in cash he stashed somewhere in Tourmaline. Fith's last words were 'the loft,' and I'll be fucked if I can figure out where the fucking loft is.

Stopping the flow of guns out of Tourmaline wasn't easy. I nearly lost my presidency over it, but surprisingly, Kade helped me to cover it up. He spends most of his time in Tourmaline now, searching for the money. He also diverted the gun-running business to another chapter of the club. I'd be happier if we got out of it altogether, and he knows it. Kade's not fucking stupid. He knows running guns is profitable, but he also knows the chances of getting caught are way too fucking high. Too many people to turn on you. Too many people to fuck things up.

When I enter my bedroom, my woman is fast asleep in the middle of the bed. Smiling at her sleeping form, I strip off my clothes and settle under the covers with my front to her back. She stirs a little, but when I place an arm around her, Kat's breathing evens out and she goes back to sleep. Kat is the reason I need to keep my club clean so nothing can blow back on her.

As I drift off to sleep, my mind goes back to Gareth Goodman, and I know my dreams are going to be haunted by images of him trying to hurt my woman.

CHAPTER 13

GARETH GOODMAN

I'm in Tourmaline, and there are so many visitors, it's easy to blend in. I've dyed my hair, grown a beard, and I'm wearing a fat suit. I look like a good ol' boy, and no one pays me any attention.

Coming here is risky, but how can I let the love of my life marry a low-life like Reynolds? He's a criminal, he's fucked everything with an orifice, and everybody knows he's using Kat for her money.

"Hey, baby, what are you doing out here in the open?" asks my helpful accomplice, Stella.

"Just blending in, honey, just blending in." She looks around, making it obvious something is up, so I grab her with one arm and kiss her.

You can't help but feel she's been kissed a lot. She's a little too eager to please and just as easy to manipulate. All I had to do was feed her some of the bullshit they told me in the hospital, and she fell for it. Her self-esteem is shattered, she knows she's getting older, and she is desperate to get married and have a family of her own. She has a tiny house in town, it's filthy, but she doesn't have many friends, so no one drops by. I've only had to fuck her a couple of times and bolster her confidence with false flattery.

"Aren't you worried about being seen?" she questions.

"By whom, honey? I look like a respectable member of the public going for a stroll with his girl."

"You mean it? You mean it when you say I'm your girl?"

The look of desperation in her eyes is truly pitiful. "Yeah, honey, after everything you've done for me? Of course, you're my girl."

The smile on her once-pretty face becomes bigger, and we walk arm in arm down the sidewalk toward her place.

As we pass the burned-down bakery, I kiss the side of her face. "You did an excellent job on that." I point at the charred shell of the building.

"I did as you told me, baby. It was easy."

"Still, *you* did it. *You* are on your path of self-fulfillment and making great leaps and bounds in the right direction." Honestly, the way this woman eats up all that bullshit amazes me, but as I look at her, I can see her chest puff up and self-pride ooze out of her.

Pathetic.

"You really think that? You really think I'm on the right path?"

"Yes, honey. Now, what do you know about the wedding? Do you have any details?"

"The wedding? Why do you care about it? Why are we even still here, baby? We should be gone. You said we'd be drinking mojitos on the beach in Mexico by now."

I look around to make sure no one is watching, and I push her up against the side of a building, squeezing her arms tight. Through gritted teeth, I say, "You *know* why I'm still here. They have to pay for locking me up in that fucking place with those fucking people. We'll be going to Mexico, honey." I release her, and she rubs her arms. "But *not* until I'm done."

Tears well in her eyes. I smile down at her, kiss her forehead, and continue the walk to her home. Thankfully, she doesn't say another word until we get inside.

"Gareth, how am I supposed to get close to the wedding? Kat doesn't even like me."

I pick her up, put her on the kitchen table, and spread her legs. With the knife on the kitchen counter, I slice her clothes off her. I want to drive the knife into her flesh to see how she bleeds, but I need her.

"Baby, if you keep cutting my clothes, I won't have anything to wear."

I smile at her. "Maybe I want you like this all the time?"

She looks so pathetically happy as she sighs and closes her eyes. She's naked now, and her body shows the signs of a life which has been played hard. She's way too thin with old track marks on her arms. I strip down to my fat suit and pull it over my head. She opens her eyes, and I put the knife to her throat.

"Sorry, baby. I'll keep them shut."

Fucking her is much easier with her eyes shut. "You know you have to pay for that, don't you, honey?"

She frowns at me but keeps her eyes shut and nods her head slightly. Slowly, she gets down off the table and turns around. She bends over and grabs her ass cheeks, spreading herself wide. I spit on my hand and rub it over my dick. It's good she disobeyed. I can fuck her without having to get her off, which takes fucking forever, and now I can do her any way I want. Those are the rules.

CHAPTER 14

JAMIE
Drummer – The Grinders

I'm staring at the ceiling of my usual room in Dane and Kat's home. My body needs to hit the gym or go for a run, but instead, I lay here on my bed thinking about life, the universe, and everything else. When I joined The Grinders, they were well on their way to success, and my life got crazy—too many chicks, too much money, and too much of everything. I couldn't keep up.

We're lucky to have Dave as our manager. He has strict rules regarding drugs and booze. Not saying we all don't partake in some things, sometimes, but generally speaking, we're all clean. Sitting up, I place my feet on the floor. Time to work out some demons with exercise.

I unzip my suitcase, find my workout gear, and dress quickly. As I open the door, I find Kat on the other side, about to knock.

"Jesus-H-Christ, Kat! You trying to put me in an early grave?"

She giggles at me. "Sorry, Jamie, I was going to ask you if you wanted to go for a run. So, do you?"

"Yeah, babe, sounds good. I need to talk to you anyway, so let's do this."

"We have to take bodyguards, unfortunately."

"Yeah, I figured that, too," I say as I run a hand over my shaved head.

As I take her in, she's a little too thin and looks tired. We've always had a good relationship, not like the one she has with Truth, but we're close. It's good she's come to me as I have a few ideas I want to run by her.

I motion for her to lead the way, and we walk downstairs in silence. She opens the front door, and there are half a dozen men out on the veranda, and one of them is her fiancé, Dane.

"Darlin', where do you think you're going?" asks Dane.

"Thought we'd go for a run. I was going to get a few of the guys to come with."

Dane flicks his gaze to me. "Now, you know the brothers can't keep up with you for long. I'd come, darlin', but I have work to do in town."

"Kat, aren't there two treadmills downstairs? We

could both jog on those, and then if you wouldn't mind, you could spot me on the weights?"

Dane looks grateful, but Kat looks annoyed. She kisses Dane on the cheek, turns, and heads for the basement.

"I owe you for that, brother." Dane gives me a nod of appreciation.

"Weren't nothing. Is she allowed to leave the house at all?" I ask.

"I'd prefer it if she stayed here. Can you keep her occupied?"

"Yeah, man, I can do that."

I give him a chin lift and go in search of Kat. When I arrive at the gym, she's already jogging at a punishing speed on the treadmill. I walk up and press buttons on her machine until she's jogging at a reasonable pace.

"What gives, Kat?" I ask as I jog on the machine next to hers.

"I'm pissed I'm housebound. I'm pissed Gareth-fucking-Goodman is on the loose. I'm pissed I didn't get the wedding cake I wanted."

"From what I could gather from last night, I thought you liked the new cake."

"I do, but it's not the point. I picked the last cake."

"Didn't you pick the new cake?" I ask, smirking at her.

She takes the towel from around her neck, scrunches it into a ball, and throws it at me. "Jamie!

That's not the point!"

I throw the towel back at her. It hits her in the face, she trips, falls onto her ass, and the treadmill deposits her on the floor.

I rush to her side instantly. "Jesus, Kat! Are you all right?"

When I get there, she has tears in her eyes. "Is he ever going to leave me alone, Jamie?" she whispers.

"Who, babe?"

"Gareth." And there it is, the actual cause behind her tears and frustration at being housebound.

"Kat, you and he had a fairly tumultuous relationship when you were together. You probably know him better than anyone. Babe, he tried to kidnap you and kill your man. Do you think he's done with you?"

She crosses her legs and leans back, so I make myself comfortable on the floor across from her.

"No, I don't think he's done with me." I raise an eyebrow at her. "I don't think he'd be stupid enough to come after me, but I think he's smart enough to try and ruin my wedding day."

"Ahh, so that's what has got you so worked up. Babe, tell me, tell Dave, hell, tell all of us what you need done, and we'll do it. Don't watch TV, don't listen to the radio, don't do interviews, and then, baby, Gareth will not exist for any of us."

A tear rolls down her face, and she absently wipes it away. "Okay, Jamie, I can do that, but you have to promise to work out with me every day and do what I say." A small smile has crept onto her face.

"Absolutely, I'll work out with you every day and do most of what you say."

"Most?"

"Aww, baby, you didn't think I'd give in so easily, did you?"

Laughter bubbles up and out of her. "Fair enough. Now, what did you want to talk to me about?"

I stand, holding my hand out to her, and help her to her feet. "I need to exercise while we talk. Is that cool?"

"Yes, sir!" She gives me a salute and gets back on the treadmill.

I begin to jog. "Kat, I want to record another album with you and the rest of the band."

She smiles at me. "Jamie, I can't sing, remember?"

"Yeah, I know, but Truth can, and Jasmin doesn't suck at it, but you *can* play the guitar, *and* you're pretty good." She looks unconvinced, so I continue, "It could be a new sound for us, a new venture. Blair and I have pretty good exposure with *Rock Star*, so promoting it will be easy. The producers of the show will go nuts for it."

"I don't know, it's been so long."

"That's why I want to try. We could record it here, we could use the Savage Angels across the states for security when we go on tour, and we could have a whole new audience with a whole new sound."

She's nodding her head, but her face is betraying what she's thinking. She's not convinced. "What about the others? Have you talked to them?"

I shake my head. "Babe, we all know you're the heart of this band. Why do you think we haven't replaced you? There's no band without you, and you are the key to getting the others on board. It's always been this way, and it always will be. You say yes, they'll come along for the ride." I grin at her, and she smiles back.

"Can I think about it?"

"Yeah, babe, of course, and I have some ideas for the new sound I want us to play with."

"How long have you been thinking about this?"

"Now, my princess of rock, we've all been thinking about this for a while now." We both turn, and Truth is slouching against the far wall. He has a knowing smile plastered on his face.

"Oh, really now?" she asks.

"It is something we've talked about over the last few years. It's time, Kat, but we won't, can't, do it without you." Kat tilts her head to the side, listening intently. "Having said that, no pressure from me or..." and I motion to Truth, "... him or any of us. These next few days are all about *you*, baby. We can go back over this after the wedding, the honeymoon, all of it. Okay?"

"Okay, Jamie. Truth, you going to work out or stand there and watch us?" she questions.

"As pleasant a sight as it is to watch you jog and everything moves up and down, I need to get some exercise in."

"This is like old times when we were on tour. Now, all we need is a hungover Jasmin to wander through the door with Blair and Curtis telling us they can't possibly work out 'cause they need to look after her." Kat laughs at the memory.

As if on cue, Jasmin walks in. She's wearing a tracksuit, sits on one of the exercise bikes, and starts pedaling. All three of us laugh, and Jasmin looks at us in confusion.

"What's so funny?" asks Jasmin.

"What are you doing?" Kat questions.

"What does it look like I'm doing?" Jasmin says in a haughty tone.

"It looks like you're exercising, but we all know you don't do that," says Truth.

She pedals harder. "No, I never used to, but last year, in three months, I put on fifteen pounds. It took me another six months to work it off. I'm not going to go through that again. So, I do thirty minutes of exercise every day, and my weight stays the same. Well, so long as I don't overindulge."

All three of us go quiet and exchange looks. This is a side to Jasmin none of us have ever seen. She's always been the live-life-to-the-fullest-and-die-young-leaving-a-good-looking- corpse-behind type. Truth starts first with a small laugh, then me, and finally, Kat.

"Yeah, yeah, bitches, laugh it up. But I *will not* get fat!" says Jasmin, with no small amount of indignation in her voice.

We all continue to exercise in silence, and I get lost in my thoughts, thinking about old times and the direction I want the band to take. We're like a family, a dysfunctional family, but we work.

CHAPTER 15

TRUTH

The four of us work out in silence for half an hour. I'm surprised Jamie talked to Kat about getting the band back together. Out of all of us, I figured they'd pick me for that conversation. I'm glad Jamie did it, though. It might just be the push Kat needs.

"Truth? Truth, are you listening?" asks Jasmin.

"What is it, my tantalizing temptress?" I look up to see her pouting at me.

"Do you ever listen when I'm talking?"

"I'm in the exercising zone, Jas. What's up?"

"What I was saying was, I need to go into town and did anyone want to come with me?"

She has a look on her face I can't quite decipher. "Sounds like fun. You'll buy me lunch?"

Relief washes over her features. "I think I can

manage lunch."

"Fuck me! Did Jasmin just offer to pay for lunch? Well, can I come, too?" Jamie chuckles.

"No, you can't, it's me and Truth. You had your chance."

"Aww, come on, Jas, I didn't know lunch was on the table," whines Jamie.

"You heard the lady, Jamie, it's Jas and me. You can come next time." I wink at him, and he gives me a huge grin.

"Cool, a threesome next time. I'm in," he replies with a chuckle. Kat nearly chokes on her water, and I grab Jasmin's hand and leave the gym.

"You all right?" I ask.

"What? Can't I want to spend time with you without the others?"

"Jezebel, Jas, you haven't spent time alone with me in a *very* long time."

"Well, today we're changing that. Give me thirty minutes to get cleaned up, and I'll meet you out front."

"Cool. See you in thirty."

Well, something is up. I watch her walk away and wonder why she wants to be alone with me. Jasmin and I have flirted with each other over the years, and at one time, I thought we'd make a good couple, but Dave made it clear if it all went south, we'd still have to work together, and it could get messy. I was still up for it, but Jas ran a mile, she wasn't willing to fuck up a good thing and put the band in jeopardy. I was mad at her for a time, but it was years ago, and we've both had numerous relationships since then.

Rubbing my face with my hands, I head upstairs. When I get to my room, I feel a hand on my shoulder.

"Hey, there, Truth."

"Judge, how's it hanging, man?"

"Well, now, that's what I wanted to talk to you about. I heard you and Jasmin are going into town together," he pauses, then squares his shoulders. "Is there something I should know?"

"Judge, she asked me into town, and we're going to have lunch, that's all. So, tell me, is there something *I* should know?"

His lips pull together in a hard line. "She's not her usual self. I could hear you two downstairs, and I thought…"

I shake my head at him. "No, and I mean *no*, man. Can't fuck someone you work with. It gets too messy. Jasmin and I flirt a lot, but you know I do that with everyone, yeah?"

"Yeah," Judge replies, as he pins me with a look.

"Man, I swear." I put one hand over my heart. "Now, I need to get changed. We cool?"

"Yeah, Truth, we're cool. But…" he leans into me, his eyes never leaving mine. "You remember whose woman she is."

With that, he turns on his heel and heads back down the hallway. That's all I need, a biker who thinks I'm messing with his woman. Opening my door, I head for the bathroom.

Today is going to be interesting.

Tourmaline has a couple of decent places to get a meal, but the best in town is Bettie's Café. Unfortunately, the town is full of new people, and as Jasmin and I sit in a booth, I feel like a fish in a goldfish bowl. Rosie, the cute waitress, has already taken our order. Bettie's packed, and the bodyguards at the door aren't letting anyone else in.

"Joyful. Jas, I think we should go. Too many crazies here. Let's go down to the Savage Angels bar. At least there we can be alone."

"I haven't eaten anything yet," she pouts.

"Well, let's get it to go and eat at the bar."

"Judge might be there."

"Yes, and the last time I checked, you and he were an item, or at least fuck buddies?" I make it a question and raise an eyebrow at her.

She frowns and says, "Yeah, we are. I need a little

space. I need to think, that's all."

"Jasmin, we've been working together for years, and I'd like to think we're friends. I know I tease you *a lot,* but you invited me out for a reason, so spill, my jolly Jas." A small smile flickers across her face at my silly play of her name.

"I'm nearly thirty."

I burst out laughing, and she scowls at me. "You're a couple of years away from that, and who cares?"

"Don't you ever think about family, marriage, and settling down?" she says in a serious tone.

"Fuck." I scrub a hand through my hair. "Your biological clock has plenty of time, you—"

"That's not what I'm talking about!" She throws a scrunched-up napkin at me. "I'm talking about finding someone. Someone to share your life with, the ups, the downs, and all the crap in between."

Now, I get it. The wedding. "Jas, you and me, we're the same." Her eyes widen, but before she can speak, I continue, "Kat was always going to get married, and I think Blair and Jamie will, too. I know Curtis has been married more times than any of us care to think about, but he's like us, too. We're going to have a different kind of normal. Well, Curtis will if he ever stops getting married to heinous bitches."

"What the fuck do you mean?"

"Love it when you talk dirty to me." I get up, sit

next to her, and put my arm around her shoulders. "Jas, do you like being with Judge?"

She nods her head, "Yes, but—"

"No buts, baby. People like you and me, we need to find happiness where we can get it, and it doesn't have to be the white picket fence and the two point three kids. I'm not saying we can't have that, but what I'm saying is, we'll have a different version of that. Does Judge make you happy?"

"We don't exactly talk a lot, but we fuck a lot."

"So, start a dialogue, feel him out. I have a feeling he'll be happy to be tied to you for a while."

"What does that mean?"

I smirk at her. "It means he may have reminded me..." and I use my fingers as inverted commas, "...whose woman you are."

"What?" Her smile grows, and she looks happy.

"Yeah, the man likes you."

"What were his exact words?"

"Nah, not doing that, Jas. Go start a conversation with him. Now, can we please get food to go and go to the bar?"

"Yeah, baby, we can."

Getting up, I move to the counter. "Hey, Rosie, could we have our order to go, please?"

"Sure thing!" replies a flustered Rosie. She always goes bright red whenever I talk to her.

"So, are you going to Kat's wedding?" I ask her.

"Yes, she's invited just about everybody in town.

It's so nice of her." She tugs on her ear nervously.

"Who are you going with?" I ask.

"Oh, I don't have a plus one." Her blush goes a deeper shade of red. "A group of us are going to go together, but no, I don't have a date."

"Cool, I don't have a date either. Maybe you could save me a dance?"

I think she's stopped breathing, and she's staring at me with a look of shock on her face.

"Really?" she squeaks out.

"Yeah, Rosie. You're my favorite waitress, after all."

I know I shouldn't be flirting with her, she's young and has a huge crush on me, but I like her. She's always happy and remembers how I like my coffee and eggs. What more can a man ask for?

She stammers out, "O-Okay, I can. I c-can save you a dance."

I wink at her and go back to Jasmin.

"Do you know she's the only person you don't give pet names to?"

"What are you talking about?" I frown at her.

"Well, my titillating Truth, you *don't* give her pet names."

She's right, I don't, and I have no idea why. "Whatever, you ready to blow this joint or what?"

I stand and help Jasmin to her feet. Rosie hands me our order, and we make our way to the front of the café.

"You ready to face the hordes of fans?" I ask.

Jasmine looks at me, smiles, and yells, "Rock-and-roll, baby!"

CHAPTER 16

STELLA

Gareth has made it very clear I have to get close to Kat Saunders, but there's only one minor problem. Kat Saunders doesn't like me. How am I supposed to get close to her, and how is this helping me on my path to self-fulfillment? All I know is, I want Gareth, and Gareth needs me to do this, and I'll do anything to make him happy.

One of the Savage Angels members was going out to Dane's, so I hitched a ride with him from Tourmaline. Now, I'm standing at the bottom of the steps leading up to his home. I've never been inside, and my stomach is in knots at the very thought of climbing the stairs and knocking on the door.

"Hey, Stella, what brings you out here?" asks a very jovial Bear. He's Road Captain of the Savage

Angels and one of the few members I haven't had sex with.

"Hey, Bear, I was wondering if Kat or Dane need any help with the wedding? I saw the bakery had burned down, and I have a cousin in Pearl County who makes cakes, and I thought..." He's staring at me as though I have two heads. "Never mind, this is a bad idea." I turn to leave.

"No, no, wait. That's real nice of you, Stella. Let me go get Kat."

Bear goes inside the beautiful house, and hard as I try, I can't get myself to walk up the stairs. I've had sex with Dane Reynolds, but he made it clear I was nothing more than a one-time fuck. Since Kat's been on the scene, he hasn't even looked at another woman.

I'm wearing a pair of jeans and a t-shirt which goes down over my butt. Not my usual dress code. I prefer it shorter, tighter, and more revealing, but Gareth said Kat might relate to me better if I dressed a little more conservatively.

With my back to the house, I'm thinking of leaving when a voice makes me turn back around.

"Hey, Stella, what can I do for you?" asks Kat.

She looks amazing. Her hair is really long, and she's wearing it over one shoulder with a black halter top and jeans on.

"Hey, Kat, I heard about the bakery, and..." She walks down the stairs toward me. "I have a cousin in Pearl County who makes cakes, and I thought if you needed someone, I could call her..." I drag out the last word and look at the ground. This is the worst idea, there's no way Kat Saunders is going to speak to me, let alone want my help with her wedding. Gareth is wrong. She won't want my help. I'm staring at my boots and realize she hasn't said anything. Slowly, I raise my eyes to hers.

She places her hand on my shoulder and says, "Thank you, Stella, it's really nice of you, but my manager has already found me a replacement."

"Oh, okay, of course, well, umm... I'll be going then," I mumble, feeling like a fool.

"You want to come in and have a coffee with me? I have some friends, well, they're more like family inside, and they don't bite much." Laughing, she reaches down and grabs my hand.

"I don't want to intrude, you probably have a million things to do, I'll just—"

"Nonsense, come on in. I need coffee. Have you had anything to eat? I could fix you something?"

"Food? Kat, are you making food? Please make it something sweet. I need some sugar!" says a very pregnant Emily as she waddles up the path from the cabins toward us.

Kat laughs louder. "Yeah, baby, I can do sweet. How do waffles sound?"

"Yay! Waffles! Let's do it."

Emily pushes between us and links her arms

through both of ours. "Okay, ladies, you now get to help me up the stairs."

I look at Kat, who shakes her head. "Are you sure I'm not imposing? I don't want to be any trouble."

"Nonsense! What's another mouth to feed? Kat, you don't mind, do you?" inquires Emily.

"Em, I was the one who invited Stella. You, on the other hand, invited yourself."

"Pfft," says Emily, waving a hand in the air. "Let's get me up these freaking stairs!"

When we get to the top of the stairs, Emily goes inside, and we follow her to the back of the house. I've never been inside Dane's house before, and it's gorgeous, with wooden floors and lots of photos on the walls. I stop to admire a few and a group photo catches my eye. It's a photo of some of the Angels, and I'm in it.

"I took that one. Hope you don't mind. You look good in it." Kat smiles.

"Why do you have it up?"

I'm so confused. *Why would she have a picture of me up in her home?*

"Well, it's a picture of the Angels, and you're part of the MC. This group of pictures is all part of the MC. I have brothers up there, and it wouldn't be complete without the Angels." She's smiling at me, grabs my hand, and tugs me further down the hallway.

The kitchen's enormous, and off it is a big deck.

I've been told how nice Dane's house is, but I never imagined it was *this* beautiful. Emily has her back to us and is standing in front of the open refrigerator.

"So, Kat, what do you need?" yells Emily.

"Em, we're right here. I need you to get out of the kitchen and go sit down. What would you like to drink?"

Emily waddles over to the dining table and slowly lowers her body onto a dining chair. "There are so many things I can no longer drink. Coffee gives me wicked heartburn, and I'll not even tell you what happens when I drink tea," she sighs heavily. "Water, could I please have water?"

"Sure, honey. How about you, Stella?"

"Do you mind if I drink coffee?" I ask Emily.

"No, I love the smell, it just doesn't love me if I drink it." She smiles at me, and it's genuine. I have no idea why these women are being nice to me. I don't have any close female friends. I never have.

"Coffee, it is!" says Kat as she pours two cups.

"I don't think I've ever seen you out here before, Stella. So, what brings you here?"

Before I can answer, Kat does, "Stella heard about my wedding cake and offered to help, but Dave has already fixed *that* problem for me."

Kat hands Emily a glass of water and goes back into the kitchen. "Are there other problems with the wedding?" I ask.

"It has been decreed from up above. I'll stay in this house until the big day." She cracks eggs into a bowl. "How am I supposed to make sure all the little things are done if I can't see it for myself?"

"I could help," I blurt out.

"Thanks, Stella, but Dave said he'd oversee everything."

"Yeah, but he's a *man*. I can give you a female perspective."

"Well, Dave *is* a man, but he's *not* a typical man. He, well, he bats for the other team."

Emily bursts out laughing. "Kat, a person would have to be blind not to have noticed, but he's still a man. I wouldn't mind, really, I'm happy to help." I know I sound desperate, and try to smile, but I'm sure it looks forced.

Kat and Emily exchange a glance, and I think I've overplayed my hand when Kat says, "That's real nice of you, Stella. I guess a female perspective would be good."

"Excellent! I'll get started on it straight away," I gush at her.

"What are you going to get started on straight away, Stella? Let me guess the newest prospect in the MC?" I swivel in my seat to see Dirt. He's Sergeant-at-Arms with the MC and not my biggest fan.

"Dirt! I can't believe you said that! Stella has been nice enough to offer to help me with the wedding, seeing as I'm stuck out here!" says a very annoyed Kat.

"Aww, Kat, Stella knows I'm only teasing, don't you, Stella?"

"Sure, sure, Dirt. I need to be going, so could you take me back into town?"

"Stella, please don't go. It's the first time we've had a genuine conversation. I'd really love to go over some of the wedding details if you have time?" says Kat.

I nod at her. "W-Well, I haven't had waffles yet, so I guess I could stay for a while." Dirt looks surprised, and Kat's smile becomes bigger. "Could you please take me back into town when we're done?" I ask Dirt.

"Yeah, I can do that. Kat, you call me when you're finished with her, okay?"

When she's finished with me?

He makes me sound like a piece of meat. Rage festers inside me, but outwardly I smile at him. He winks at me and goes back outside to the deck where there is half-dozen or so members.

I can't hear what's being said, but all the brothers are staring at me and laughing.

"Don't pay him any attention, Stella. You know how grumpy he can get," says Kat.

"Yeah, I know how he can be. So, how many people have you invited to the wedding?"

"Too many. Last count was two hundred and

thirty-eight, and not all of them have RSVP'd. The wedding planner still needs to follow up with another fifty or so people. Hopefully, it'll be done today, so we'll have definite numbers."

"Okay, what can I do? The wedding is in the church in town, and the reception is in the Town Hall, right?" I ask.

Emily blurts out, "And the park in front of the Town Hall. The very cute town mayor said she could have that, too. Hey, is he single?"

"Emily, why would you care if he was single or not?" laughs Kat.

"A woman can dream," replies Emily.

Kat shakes her head at her and rolls her eyes. "The town mayor is single, but he's married to this town. His family was one of the first to settle here in Tourmaline. They've always served the town in one form or another."

"More like they think they own the town," I say. Both women stare at me. "I know he's easy on the eyes, but he's tried to make trouble for the MC in the past. He can't be trusted."

"I know he's been less than helpful in the past, but he's been working with the MC for the betterment of the town." She looks a little annoyed, and Emily looks uncomfortable.

"Yeah, I can see how you'd say that. Of late, he has been nicer to us."

Kat pours batter into a waffle iron and asks, "Em,

how many waffles?"

"A lot."

I laugh at her, and Kat smiles. "Getting back to the wedding, can I help with anything at the Town Hall or the church?" I ask.

"There is one thing. I want it to be pretty. Could you confirm the number of tables at the Town Hall and pews at the church? And make sure I have enough bows and flowers to decorate it all?"

I give her my biggest smile. "Absolutely! Will they give me access to them?"

"I'll make sure, love. I'll call the minister and Justice."

"I'll do it as soon as I get back into town."

"Enough wedding talk! Those waffles are mine! Stella, you'll have to wait," says Emily.

"Em! She's our guest!"

"What? I'm hungry." She looks innocently at Kat.

I laugh out loud at these women. It's obvious they're very close.

"Don't laugh at her, Stella, you're only encouraging her. I swear, you get bossier with every pregnancy."

"No, it's every year I spend with Sal. The man is nothing *but* bossy."

We all burst out laughing, and I realize Kat Saunders isn't anything like I thought she was.

CHAPTER 17

ADELYNN

Jonas is standing in the enormous kitchen of this lovely home. It's got four bedrooms, two bathrooms, and sits on five acres of land. It's more than we need, and the real estate agent is looking at us expectantly.

"Well, folks, what do you think? It's not too far out of town, and the aspect is perfect. The back patio area will catch the winter sun."

"I like it, Addy. What do you think? Do you think Ben will like it?"

"Jonas, Ben will love it, but how much is this to rent?" I ask.

The agent replies, "No, this isn't for rent. I'm sorry, Mr. White, I thought you wanted to look at places for sale? It's under the budget you gave me, and it has been on the market for a while. I could ask if they want to rent it, but I don't think they will."

"Could you give us a minute?" asks Jonas.

"Of course, I'll be out front. You folks take your time." He gives us both a big grin and leaves.

"Jonas, what's going on?"

He walks up to me and grabs me around the waist. I'm tall, but he's taller, so I crane my neck back to look at him. His smile looks contrite, and he places his forehead against mine, cupping my face with his hands.

"Love, I meant it when I said I wanted to make a go of it. I thought we could buy this place together. I thought this could be our home... yours, mine, and Ben's."

He picks me up and puts me on the kitchen bench, then positions himself between my legs. He looks so happy, and things have been good between us, but this is a tremendous step for me.

"Jonas, I don't know. Renting is one thing, but buying a home together? That's more than we talked about."

He places his hands on my thighs and says, "Love, it's no different. I'm simply putting down roots in a permanent kind of way. There's no pressure on you. I'll pay for it. I want you to know I'm serious, that for me, this is it. I want you and no one else."

I'm staring into his gorgeous green eyes, trying to see if he's really changed, and so far, everything he has said and done should prove it to me. But buying a house together? That's an enormous commitment.

"Are you going to speak, love, or should I try to persuade you with sexual-fucking- advances?" His eyes sparkle with mischief, and his hands work their way up my thighs.

"Jonas, there's a man waiting outside for us—"

"We can be quiet. I could gag you again." He cocks an eyebrow at me.

Desire pools between my legs. This man has always had too much power over me.

"Jonas! Step back, let me think for a minute."

"Fuck that, no thinking, let's feel for a minute 'cause, love, you know I can make you feel good."

He kisses me, and his hands travel over my body. My arms wind around him, and my hands entangle in his hair. I'm lost in him. It's always been like this.

"Say yes, Addy. Let's start our life together properly, here, in this house with a kitchen counter that's the right height for fucking."

Laughter escapes me. "Jonas!"

"Do you like the house? Do you want me?" His eyes are searching mine, and he looks a little conflicted.

"It's not that I don't want you or this lovely house. What if things between us go bad? What if you wake up one day and don't want me?"

"Not going to happen, but I see what you're saying. *If* it happens, I'll sell, you go your way, and I'll go mine. But I repeat, it's *not* going to happen. I lost you once, I'm *never* losing you again."

Damned if I don't believe him. After all we've been through, we deserve our piece of happiness.

Kissing him, I pull back to ask, "Can we take another look at the master bedroom and check out the fucking height in the bathroom?"

His grin widens, and laughter rumbles out of his chest. "Does it all come down to the fucking height in the bathroom? 'Cause if it does, love, I can always get it remodeled. Another selling point is all the other bedrooms are at the other end of the house, so you can be as noisy as you'd like." He winks at me, helps me down, and places his hand in mine, guiding me to the main bedroom.

CHAPTER 18

SHERIFF CARLOS MORALES

My office is my haven from the public and from the other officers who work for me. I see the whole bullpen from my desk and know most of my men so well. Their facial expressions usually tell me what they're thinking. I'm staring at Officer Barrett, and he looks concerned as he speaks into the telephone. His eyes lock with mine, and shock washes across his features. I stand, but he raises a hand to stop me from continuing. He hangs up the phone and comes to me.

I meet him at my door. "Billy, you all right?"

"Sheriff, that was a tip about the Savage Angels having a shipment of drugs in their compound here in Tourmaline."

"From whom?" I've never liked the MC, but as far

as I can tell, they have never run anything out of Tourmaline.

"He wouldn't leave his name, told me to look in Dane Reynolds' room at the compound and that Reynolds is there right now."

"You think it's legit?" He shrugs at me. "We have to go check it out. You go to the courthouse and see if you can get a warrant. In the meantime, I'll ask if I can take a look around," I say.

"They've never done anything like this before, Sheriff. I can't believe with the wedding so close they'd start now."

"I agree with you, but it's the perfect cover, isn't it?" I reach for my hat and get my gun out of my desk. "If they agree to me having a look around, then I'm thinking it's a bogus call from one of the reporters in town trying to drum up a story."

"You want me to hold off on the warrant then, Sheriff? I could come with you?"

I look Barrett up and down. My logic tells me it's a hoax, but I nod at him. "Yeah, Billy, if they refuse, I'll wait in the bar for you to get back with a warrant."

"Okay, Sheriff."

"Go get your hat. You can drive, and we'll take my cruiser. I'll meet you out front."

As I stand out on the sidewalk and look up and down Main Street, I'm surprised at the amount of activity in town. It's normally only like this when it's snow season.

There's a commotion down near Bettie's Café, and I see two people being ushered into a car. No doubt they are some of Kat's celebrity friends being harassed by their waiting fans.

Barrett appears beside me, and we both climb into the cruiser. The car the people got into is going in the same direction as we are and even pulls into the Savage Angels' compound. As soon as we drive through, the gates close behind us. I watch as Truth and Jasmin get out of the car, laughing.

Truth makes his way toward us, and when I get out of the car, he yells, "Sheriff, we didn't need a police escort. We're safe here. Thanks, anyway!"

"Don't flatter yourself, Truth, I'm here on official business."

He feigns a look of hurt. "Aww, Sheriff, you wound me."

"Somehow, I think it would take more than *that* to wound you," I respond.

He chuckles, and Jasmin laughs as we all head into the clubhouse. Once inside, I see Dane sitting at the bar with Kade, and they look deep in conversation. Kade says something to Dane and motions his head in our direction. Dane swivels in his chair.

"Dane! Our host with the most! The sheriff here needs an official word with you," says Truth.

"Thank you, Truth. What would we do without

you?" I ask.

He again feigns another look of hurt and walks up to the bar. "Could we please have two glasses and a bottle of Fireball, unless you'd like to join us, Sheriff, Deputy?"

"Official business, remember?" I say, with a hint of humor in my voice. Truth is flamboyant and tries to play the bad-boy card, but to me, he's comical. I'd be surprised if anyone took him seriously.

"Truth, leave the sheriff alone. Let's eat and drink," Jasmin says, smiling at me.

I smile at her and then give Dane Reynolds my full attention. "Dane, can I speak to you privately?"

"Sure, Sheriff." He gets up and opens the door to their meeting room. "In here, okay?"

"Yes. Billy, could you wait out here, please?"

"Sure, Sheriff." He doesn't look happy, but I want a private word with Dane before we ask if we can look around. I was a detective in a big city for years, and reading people is second nature to me. If he's lying, I should be able to tell from his body language and the tone of his voice.

Dane gives Billy a quizzical look, but he looks at the floor. I've often wondered if there's a connection between them, but I've never been able to prove it. Until then, I keep Billy around. He's a good officer, level-headed, and eager to learn. If he stays clean and out of trouble, he'll make a good sheriff one day.

Dane walks into the room and leans against the table. "So, what can I do for you, Sheriff?"

"Dane, we've had a tip at the station. It seems someone thinks you have a shipment of drugs in your room here at the compound."

He buckles over with laughter and slowly stops when he realizes I'm not laughing. "Fuck me, Carlos, you're serious? You know I'm not stupid enough to run anything out of Tourmaline, especially so close to my wedding with half the fucking country in my backyard," he growls at me.

"Then, you won't mind us taking a look around."

His eyes blaze with anger, he straightens up, and I subconsciously place my hand on my gun. He looks at me and shakes his head.

"Fuck it. Fine, go through my room, go through the entire fucking clubhouse. Hell, check the garage and offices, too. 'Cause, Sheriff, if I'm fucking stupid enough to have anything here, I deserve to get caught."

He walks past me into the bar area and whistles, long and loud. "Listen up, everyone outside! The sheriff is going to search the premises. Let's give him plenty of room and let him do his fucking job!" He pins me with a look and walks outside.

They file past me, making snide remarks, and I wait until the only people left in the clubhouse are myself, Billy, Truth, and Jasmin.

"What the fuck, Sheriff? You know Dane isn't a

douchebag. You know his club keeps it clean in Tourmaline," says Jasmin as laughter bubbles up and out of her. "Hey, I'm a poet, and I didn't know it! Seriously, though, Kat is going to pitch a fit when she finds out you did this."

"We got a tip. It's his job, Ma'am," replies Deputy Barrett.

Truth snorts and slaps the table. "Sheriff, you're one of the few people in this town who knows his ass from his elbows. Do you really think the Savage Angels or Dane would do anything that could blow back on Kat? You know he fucking adores her. You'd have to be blind not to see it. Even the wedding... how many of the MC have had a traditional wedding in this town? I'm guessing the answer is zero."

"You're right, but I can't take his or *your* word for it. I *do* have a job to do, and I'm going to do it." I nod at Deputy Barrett, and we both walk toward the private rooms at the back of the clubhouse.

Jasmin yells out, "His is the third door on the right, unless you're going to search all of them?"

I open the door and look in. There's not a lot in there. It's got a bed, a chest of drawers, and a built-in closet with a bathroom off to one side. Billy goes into the room, but I stay in the hallway. I know there's nothing in here, and I really don't want to go through Dane and Kat's things.

"Sheriff, where should I start?"

"We both know this is bullshit, don't we?"

"Ahh, yes, Sheriff, we do, but we can't ignore a tip."

I sigh, take my hat off, and scratch my head. "Come on, Billy, let's get out of here. We shouldn't have come."

"Sheriff, I taped the call. Maybe we can trace it?"

"You could have told me that *before* we left the station, Billy. Let's follow that down and get the fuck out of here." I turn to leave, and Dane Reynolds is standing beside me with his arms crossed.

"If you thought it was bullshit, why are you here?" he demands.

"I have a job to do."

"Yeah, so why aren't you doing it?" He folds his arms flex across his chest and doesn't look happy.

"Someone is causing you grief before your wedding day, and everyone knows I have a bug up my ass for the MC." Dane raises his eyebrows at me and places his hands on his hips. "I'm sorry. It's *your* wedding that is making the entire town crazy. Maybe we should re-name it Savage Town?" I sigh and hold out my hand.

He grasps my hand and chuckles. "Savage Town? I like it."

"Not going to happen, Reynolds, and thank you for not being a dick."

He gives me a chin lift and goes to the front of the clubhouse.

"Come on, Billy, let's trace the call and listen to the tape."

"You sure, Sheriff?"

"Yeah, Billy, let's roll."

CHAPTER 19

KAT

It's late at night, and Dane still isn't home. I'm sitting at the kitchen table when Dirt comes into the room. He smiles at me, walks over to the coffee maker, and holds up a cup.

"Yeah, honey, that would be nice." He pours two cups, walks over, and sits down next to me, handing me one of the mugs. I study his face as we sit in silence, sipping our coffee. When we first met, one of the first things I noticed about him was the scar that runs up his face and into his hairline. But now, I don't even notice it. Dirt isn't what you would call handsome—he's more rugged or well-lived. He's loyal to Dane and the MC, and as I'm Dane's woman, he's protective of me. I know he and my ma were friends, and she helped him in some kind of way.

Apart from saying he liked her apple muffins, he doesn't talk about her much.

"Kat, what did Stella want?" he asks.

"I know it's weird. She offered to help me with finding a new wedding cake."

"You've already got that sorted." He stares at me intently.

"Dirt, I know you don't like her, but maybe she's finally realized I'm not going anywhere. I think she's really trying to befriend me, and I think it's nice."

He snorts and looks at his coffee cup. "Kat, women like Stella don't have women friends. It's too much competition for them. She's been around the club a long time, but she's poison. You need to keep away from her."

"Wow, that's harsh… poison? She's trying really hard and for what? I'm not paying her, she's only doing it to be nice." I was surprised when Stella came out here and offered to help, and there isn't anything in it for her except to get on my good side and maybe be my friend.

"Okay, be careful, and if you need anything, you call me, yeah?"

"All right, I'll be careful, but what's she going to do? Attack me with a cake?"

"That woman is manipulative. Don't let her get too close, don't let her in…" He taps my chest, "… here."

"Dirt, what's gotten into you tonight?"

"It's strange, after all this time, she's trying to make amends, that's all." He shakes his head as though he doesn't believe it.

"As I said, maybe she's realized I'm staying." I give him my best smile, but he frowns at me.

"Kat, from the moment I saw you and Dane together, I knew you'd be around forever. The way you two are with each other, you'd have to be a moron not to see it. If she's only just figured that out, it's another reason to steer clear of her."

I stand and take my half-drunk coffee to the sink and pour it down the drain. "All right, Dirt, I'll be careful. Do you know why Dane isn't home yet?" I ask, hoping to change the subject.

"Club business, Kat. Is there a spare room in this house?"

"Yes, the one on this level is empty. Just in case one of you needs to stay." Smiling at him, I move back toward him and touch his shoulder. "Night, Dirt."

"Night, Kat. Sleep well."

CHAPTER 20

DAN
Lead Singer – Dark Ink

It's been *the* fucking trip from hell. I thought Amy and I could work through our problems, that the music would prevail, and we'd both put it first, but my jealousy is like a fucking bonfire. All I have to do is look at her, and it flares its ugly head again and again. Part of the problem is we're going to Tourmaline for Kat Saunders' wedding, and I know Truth will be there. Amy and Truth had a week of sexual activities a while ago. It's not that I think I can claim her, but if she's fucking me, I don't want her fucking anyone else.

We're on the cusp of making it in the music industry, with no small amount of help from The Grinders. They mention us in interviews and even come to our gigs. We owe them, but I want Amy to myself, and I do *not* want to share her with Truth.

As far as I know, it was only one week, and he keeps away from her when we are at gigs or functions, but I see her watching him, and it drives me fucking insane.

"Dude, you and Amy need to sort your shit out before we get to Tourmaline," says Everett, my lead guitarist.

I hold my head in my hands, then I scrub my face and look at him.

"I know, E, I know. This fucking tour bus isn't big enough for all of us. What the fuck was Dave thinking, making us go across the fucking country in something that isn't big enough to piss in?"

"Whoa, dude, calm the fuck down. This bus is nice compared to where I was living before I made it into the band."

Everett is tall, lanky, and he can play a mean guitar. We found him busking in the subway a few years ago, trying to earn enough money to buy himself a meal. Amy offered to buy him something to eat in exchange for him coming to auditions. He'd lived rough for a while and has always been so grateful to us for finding him. He still hasn't figured that without him, we wouldn't have a band. As soon as we heard him, we knew he was gifted, and he's done his best to fit in with the band ever since.

"Yeah, man, sorry. You're right. It's a little

claustrophobic at the moment."

"Never used to be, not until you fucked it up, anyway."

"Careful, E, you're messing with shit you have no right to mess with."

He stands and cups his hands around his mouth and yells, "Band meeting! Right now!"

"What the fuck, E?" I growl at him.

Slowly, everyone files into the lounge area of the bus, with Amy bringing up the rear. She avoids eye contact with me and sits as far away from me as she can.

E points at me and says, "You need to get yourself under control. Amy is her own person and can talk to other members of the male race. It doesn't mean she's interested in them." I stand, and my eyes blaze with anger, but before I can respond, Amy cuts me off. "He's right, Dan." My head whips around, and I stare at her with a look of disdain.

"Oh, *give me a break, Amy*. You're as much to blame as Dan is. Either you two are on or off. You can't put yourself out there as if you're single, and honey, we all know you do *that*. If you haven't figured it out, Dan is hooked, and you don't need to play hard to get anymore. You need to be a little more attentive to Dan and not the *rest* of the male population."

"Fuck you, Everett!" yells Amy and goes to leave, but he grabs her arm.

"No, this is us having a meeting, Amy, and this means you both need to sit and listen."

"Take your hands off her, E," I say in a low, commanding voice.

He immediately lets her go and puts both hands in the air.

"Could we all sit down?" This comes from our keyboard player, Craig. I raise an eyebrow at him and sit back down, and Amy does the same. "We all heard what Dave said to you in the booth. To me, it would feel like we've failed before we even started if we had to replace you, Amy."

"What the fuck are you talking about?" I ask, incredulous Dave would've said that.

"Dave basically said if you and I didn't sort this out, I'm gone. It's the reason we were made to come by bus."

All my anger leaves me. She looks sad as she makes this admission. "Why didn't you say something?"

"I've tried, but you won't listen." Her tone is flat with no emotion coming through at all.

"You should've tried harder, Amy," I say.

"Jesus, Dan, it takes two to tango, and I *tried*. You don't listen to anything I have to say, from our relationship to how I think a song should go. If I say black, you say white, and you know it!" Now, *there's* the woman I know, full of fire.

I say nothing and smile at her, which appears to

infuriate her more. She rolls her eyes and sits back further into the seat, crossing her arms and shaking her head.

"I'm with Craig on this. It would feel like we've failed, but I want this too damned much to lose it because you two can't work it out. We'll be in Tourmaline tomorrow morning, and we need to either be a band who can work together, or we need to find a new drummer," says Milo, our bass guitarist. The others all nod, and Amy's eyes shine with unshed tears.

She stands. "Dan and I will sit down and talk, and if we can't work through this, then, when we get to Tourmaline, I'll leave." Her bottom lip quivers, she turns, and walks toward the back of the bus.

Fuck! This is the last thing I need. Give me a screaming, raging Amy, but not a crying one. I have no idea how to handle this version of her. I don't think I've even seen her cry in all the time I've known her.

I sigh and take in the rest of the band, all staring at me. "All right, all right! I'll fix this. No matter what, we aren't losing Amy. I'll make this work," I grumble as I follow her retreating form.

I find her sitting on her bed, legs crossed, and her eyes closed, with her head down. When we first met, she had shaved her head, but now, she keeps it in a short bob. She has a tattoo of a music note near one of her eyes, and it sums her up beautifully. For her, music always comes first, and she's wrong. I listen to her when it comes to the music. She challenges me all the time, and I love it. I know the album we're working on is going to be huge, and that's mainly because of her and the fact she won't let me take the easy route.

Sitting next to her, I rest my elbows on my knees and lean forward. Without looking at her, I ask, "Why didn't you tell me what Dave said?" I keep my tone calm and controlled.

"I was hoping we could work things out. I didn't want you to keep me out of guilt 'cause I'm getting booted from the band. I was trying to fix it without you even knowing about it."

"I don't want you to leave the band, no matter what." I genuinely mean this. It wouldn't be the same without her.

"Dan, to be honest, we don't work, but at the same time, I don't think I could handle it if you found someone else. Not at the moment, anyway."

Her admission takes me by surprise. Glancing up at her, she returns my gaze with tears in her eyes. Something in me breaks as I watch a tear roll down her cheek. Without thought, my hand gently goes to her face, and I wipe it away. More tears fall, and I pull her to me by dragging her across my lap. She doesn't make a sound as she silently sobs.

"Please don't cry, babe. It kills me to see you cry." I kiss her neck, cheeks, nose, and then find my way to her mouth. She offers no resistance as my tongue parts her lips and duels with hers.

Placing her on the bed, I cover her body with my own as my hands roam over her, exploring her intimate places. Amy rarely wears panties, and as I pull up her skirt, I'm pleased to find she isn't wearing any. Her hands go to my belt, and she undoes my jeans. As soon as my cock springs free, she strokes me. Continuing my kisses, I trail my way down her luscious body before placing my head between her legs. A moan escapes her as I roll my tongue over her clit. She grinds into my face as I suck, lick, and explore her pussy. Grabbing me by the ears, she surprises me and pulls me up so she can kiss me. She loves oral, giving and *especially* receiving. Sometimes, it's all she wants to do.

I break away from her and move back toward her pussy when she says, "No, I want you to make love to me. I want your cock inside me, and I want it now."

Not wanting to deny her, I push my jeans further down and place my cock at her entrance, thrusting in as far as I can go within her slick, tight pussy. Slowly, I draw myself out and do it again. I place my arm under her head, grip one of her shoulders with my other hand, and begin pumping in and out of her. I'm holding her in place, and I know she doesn't like it, as she can't roll her hips. Letting me know her frustration, she bites my ear hard.

"You know I love it when you do that," I growl at her.

"Let me move, Dan. It's not all about you."

She sounds annoyed, so I stop, pull out, and rise on my elbows. "Have I ever not gotten you there?"

"Yes, the time after we played for Indie Rock."

"Babe, I was drunk, and I made it up to you." She frowns and turns her head away from me. "Look at me." She doesn't, so I put my lips on the edge of her mouth. "Tell me what you want, I'll do anything, only please, don't shut me out." There's something about her that drives me crazy.

"Let me ride you. Let's change positions."

I get off the bed and take off my shoes, then my jeans. Glancing at her, she's not looking at me and is kneeling on the bed.

"Jesus, Amy, we don't have to do this, we could simply talk." A look of surprise crosses her face. "Yes, I'm capable of a conversation." I smirk at her, and she pulls her skirt down over her knees.

"I guess I thought because we'd started, that..."

"We were friends once, remember? How about we try going back to that? No sex, no strings, just friends and the music." The last fucking thing I want is to be only a friend to her, but if I can't have her any other way, I'll take it.

"You don't listen, do you, Dan? I want to be with you, but I need a different version of us. One where you respect me and listen to what I'm saying."

"Babe, think you've got this the wrong way around." I pull my jeans back up and flop back down on her bed. "I'm not the one who carries on with every single fucker in the room."

"I have *never* cheated on you, Dan, and I'm sick of being accused of it," she says firmly.

"You may not have fucked them, Amy, but you flirt, and everyone thinks you're available. I can't deal, and I don't want to."

She sighs and grabs my hand. "Yes, I flirt, but everyone *knows* I'm with you." I give her a slight shake of my head. "I'll try harder, but I need you to try, too. Your jealousy and the way you speak to me in front of the other band members isn't cool."

For a while, we sit in silence, then she moves closer to me, tracing circles on my hand. My jealous streak is vicious and ferocious, it's something I know I need to get a better handle on. I don't like other guys looking at her or talking to her or *anything*. I have no idea how I'm supposed to handle it. I've never felt this way about another woman. This whole relationship thing is hard work.

Amy breaks the silence. "Can we try again? Can we try dating and getting to know each other? Dan, baby, I want this. I want us."

Her words cut through me. Thank fuck she wants me too. I cup her face and kiss her before lightly resting my forehead against hers.

"Dating? We've never done that," I whisper.

"No, we haven't. I expect them to be full-service dates, too."

"What's a full-service date?"

She pulls away from me with a huge grin on her face. "Well, you're the complete gentleman, pay for everything, and fuck me at the end of the night."

I laugh, push her back down on the bed, and lay beside her with my leg over her. "I pay for everything?"

"Yes, and we talk and get to know each other. For instance, what's my favorite color?"

"Hang on, *I* pay for everything?" I ask, teasing her.

"Yes, *you* pay for everything. Now answer the question."

"It's blue, but it's deep-sea blue. You think it's calming." I push her hair off her face, and she looks surprised. "What? I *do* listen when you speak."

"I..." She stops and bites her bottom lip.

"What, babe?"

"I don't know yours."

"Black."

"Black isn't a color, Dan."

"No, it's the absence of color." I grin at her.

"What does that even mean?" she asks.

"Black absorbs light, and, baby, I'm ready to absorb you."

"Are you saying I'm your light?" She giggles at me.

"My light, moon, sun, and stars," I whisper. "My everything."

She reaches up and pulls my head to hers. "I like that." Her mouth finds mine, and it's a lazy, long kiss. When we come up for air, her lips are swollen, and her eyes are filled with desire.

"You have too many clothes on, Dan."

"Yeah, and I want nothing more than to fuck you, but I think we should take this slow. Get to know each other and see what happens."

Laughter bubbles up and out of her. She wraps her arms around my back and twists, so she's on top. She undoes my jeans and reaches for my cock. Before I can even protest, she impales herself on me and moves her hips. I'm lost in her, just like every other time we've been together.

She places my hand near her clit, and I rub the small nub. Her movements become more rapid, and her moans are louder. She's very close, so I reach up and tweak her nipple, and it sends her over the edge. I can feel her sex spasm around my cock, and I place both hands on her hips, moving her faster until I reach my orgasm. It washes over me, through me, and fills up the void between us. She flops down on top of me, panting. I stroke her hair and enjoy the feeling of being inside her and holding her close.

"Dan?"

"Yeah, babe?"

"You owe me a date."

I squeeze her tight and laugh.

We have a long way to go, but this was a good beginning.

CHAPTER 21

AMY
Drummer – Dark Ink

Sex for Dan and me is like breathing. It's the one thing we can always come back to, the one thing which always works. It's the glue binding us together. I love Dan, but I'm not sure if I can or want to be tied to one person forever. We talked all night and sorted through many of our issues. He didn't come right out and say it, but I know he's concerned about Truth. He need not worry. Truth isn't interested in me anymore. In fact, as soon as our fling was over, he made it clear he didn't want a permanent relationship. Truth is, after all, a rock god and can have anyone or anything he likes.

Our tour bus has pulled up in front of The Country Inn, and we all climb out. The band is happy that Dan and I have worked it out, but my concern is I don't know how long it will last. Jumping off the last step, I raise my arms into the air and stretch. I notice Dave is waiting for us, and I walk toward him. One of his assistants was supposed to come with us across the country, but we deliberately left her behind. He does not look pleased with us if the scowl on his face is anything to go by, but I knew we needed to work through this by ourselves.

"Hello, Amy." Dave embraces me, then holds me at arm's length. "How was the trip out?"

"Good, Dave, just what the manager ordered." I smile playfully at him.

He gives me a knowing smile. "You left Veronica behind, and she isn't pleased. You made her look bad."

"I'm sorry, Dave. I knew this was something we needed to do as a band and not with an arbitrator. It's all on me, and if you want to fire my ass because of it, well, go ahead and do it." I know I may be overplaying my hand, and he does own us, but he likes to make money, and we're on the verge of making him more.

"Is it sorted, then?" he asks, still grasping my upper arms.

"Yes."

"Yes?" He lets go of me and ruffles my hair. "Good. Now, get the others and come meet the proprietor of this motel. Her name is Adelynn, and she's a good friend of the family."

The guys are all standing near the bus, and as I approach Dan, he grabs me by the hand. "So, what's the verdict? Is he cool?"

"Yeah, he's cool. Wants us to meet the owner, she's a friend of the family." I tug on his hand. "Come on, let's all play nice and put on a show for Dave."

Dan kisses my cheek, and we walk hand in hand toward Dave, who frowns at us. "Well, my Dark Ink, welcome to Tourmaline. I'm afraid you'll be sharing rooms. I only got you two, so you can argue over who's sleeping with who."

"How come you only got us two rooms?" asks Milo.

"This wedding has brought many people from all over the world to this little town. The more people who stay here, the more who might come back in the future. It's good for the economy, and the owner asked me to do it." He smiles at all of us and motions us into the office of the motel.

It takes a moment for my eyes to adjust from being in the sunlight to the shade of the office. When they do, standing in front of me is a very tall, beautiful woman with an enormous smile on her face.

"Welcome to The Country Inn and Tourmaline! My name is Adelynn, and I'm here to help you in any way I can."

We all offer an assortment of greetings, and as I look at the men in the room, I see they're all enamored with her. Then in walks an MC member, who's tall, really good-looking, and it's clear, she only has eyes for him.

"Morning, folks, name's Jonas. I'm the VP in Savage Angels. Addy and I are pleased to welcome you to Tourmaline." He embraces her from behind and kisses the side of her neck.

I look at my band, who all look disappointed, even Dan. Dave raises his eyebrows at me and shakes his head. Now wasn't the time.

"Adelynn, Jonas, thank you both for having us. Let's get them sorted, then I can take them all out to see Kat," says Dave.

"Change of plans, Dave. Addy has had a few more bookings off Kat's guest list, high-profile ones, so the band is going to stay out at Kat's old home," says Jonas.

"Why didn't Kat tell me this?" Irritation laces Dave's tone.

"As far as I know, she was going to, but you left really early this morning, and she didn't get a chance. She trusts you all will treat her home with respect, seeing as you've stayed there before. Plus, she thought it would be easier for you, Dave, to record with them."

"Yes, it will be. All right, everyone, back on the bus."

As I turn to leave the office, Dave grabs my arm. "Amy, you get to drive with me."

Great. This means Dave wants to have a private conversation with me, and I'm not sure if I'm ready to answer his questions.

"I'll come with," says Dan.

"No need, my boy, just a friendly conversation between friends," replies Dave.

"Good, then you won't mind me coming," says Dan, grabbing my other hand.

We walk outside hand in hand again, and I have to admit, I like it when Dan doesn't let me face things alone. It's nice to have someone next to you who will stand by you.

"Okay, see you all when the bus makes it out there," says a disgruntled Craig.

"Aww, come on, Craig, it'll be fun, just us three and the bus driver! If you're good, we'll crack a window for you." Everett laughs.

Milo winks at me, and we go in separate directions.

"All right, you two, my car is over here." Dave points at a black Chrysler, then leads the way.

Dave climbs into the driver's seat, and Dan opens the passenger side door for me.

"My lady." He bows and helps me into the seat, then he gets into the back and sits in the middle.

Dave starts the car and pulls out onto Main Street. "I take it you two are an item, again."

"Well, Dave, we were always an item," says Dan, with attitude dripping from every word.

"I had hoped you would put the band first and discontinue this dalliance."

"Dave, we're working on our relationship but have agreed it will never affect the band ever again. We want this too much, and we need you to help us get there." He keeps his face a mask of neutrality. I glance at Dan, who shrugs at me. "Dave, we need you to be okay with this."

"So long as I never have to watch another temper tantrum between the two of you, I'll be happy."

"Dave, we aren't promising not to do that. We argue over the music all the time, but from now on, we won't bring our personal issues into it... well, we'll try not to, anyway," says Dan, trying to sound sincere. I smile at him, and Dan leans forward and tweaks my nose as a giggle escapes me.

"All right then, I'm holding you both to that. We'll get you all settled at Kat's, then you can come see her at Dane's. Keep away from the reporters and no interviews *at all*, okay?"

Dave sounds more relaxed, and it's all business now.

"Why no interviews? Surely, it's good exposure for us?" I ask.

"There's more going on than you know, and I

don't want to whip them into more of a frenzy than they already are."

He pulls up in front of Kat's house, winds down his window, and punches the code in for the gate. It slowly opens, and he drives through. Dan gets out and opens my door as Dave opens the house up for us.

"You okay?" asks Dan.

"Yes, and thank you for coming with me. I didn't really want to face Dave on my own, he can be scary."

Dan chuckles at me. "Yes, he can be." He pulls me into him and kisses me, sending electric pulses to all of my nerve endings. I pull away when I hear the bus pull into the driveway.

"You better go let them in," I say to him.

He kisses me again and runs toward the gate while I walk inside to find Dave. He's sitting in the booth of the recording studio, and I sit beside him.

"For the first time in a long time, I'm unsure what to do." He looks at me. "Sexual relationships in bands rarely end well. Do I cut you now? Or do I wait for you and Dan to implode? Then, it's all over for all of us."

"It's not going to be a problem. We've talked for hours about what will happen if anything goes wrong. We'll figure it out."

"Yes, until he pisses you off again, and you flutter your eyelashes at the nearest male," retorts Dave.

"No, I'm not going to do that, only on stage with the audience. Never again in a personal setting."

He laughs, but there's no humor in his voice. "Amy, his jealous streak is going to be your undoing, and we both know it. He's too young to keep it under control. How are *you* going to handle that?"

"We've talked it through, Dave. We know our problems. Please don't cut me, please let's see how this all plays out. Give me a year to see if we can do this." I'm pleading with him, hoping he'll let me stay. Music and the band are the only things I have ever wanted, but to get Dan in the package as well would be a dream come true.

"Six months, Amy. If you guys can keep it together for that long, then we'll revisit this subject and decide then. Fair?"

"Fair." He stands and holds out a hand to me.

"Let's go get your bags and put them in your room. I want to get back to Kat."

"Hey, Dave. How's it going?" says Everett as the band walks through the door.

"Dave, we've been trapped in a bus for ages. Why don't you go back to Kat, and we'll take the track at the rear of the house and walk over?" I suggest.

"Done! Enjoy your walk. See you in an hour, yes?" With a smile and a wave, he's gone.

The guys all look at me. "What?"

"An hour?" They all say at once.

I burst out laughing. "Yes, an hour, the exercise will do us good."

"Damn, woman, it's just as well you can play the drums well," says a disgruntled Milo.

I laugh at him. "Come on, let's go get our bags, and I call dibs on the room at the back. It has the best view."

"No fair! Some of us have never stayed here before!" cries Everett.

"You snooze, you lose." I slap his chest on the way back out to the bus.

The driver already has all our bags out of the bus and on the ground. Walking up, I grab mine and head back inside. The largest room also has the best view and it's at the back of the house. I open the door, and thankfully no one has claimed it. I'm unpacking when Dan comes into the room.

"Is it cool if I stay in here with you?"

"Yeah, babe, I'd like that."

I really wanted to have some alone time before we meet up with Kat and The Grinders, well, Truth. Dan's insecurities about him will be a test, and it will be in front of Dave, so I wanted to make sure he knows I'm committed to him and our band.

"You going to be okay when we meet up with... The Grinders?" I tentatively ask.

He stops what he's doing and sits on the bed with his back to the headboard. "Not going to lie to you, babe, I'm not looking forward to it." The frown on his face is evidence of that.

"We could always bail, stay here, and send the guys off on their own?"

"Do you really think they'd be able to follow the path to find Kat's new home?" he asks.

I giggle. "You have a point, but if you're going to feel uncomfortable or anything, babe, I'm happy for them to try."

"Everett gets lost with a GPS."

We both burst out laughing. It's true. I've never met anyone who can distrust technology so much he ends up in the complete opposite direction.

"Amy, do you love me?" I look over, and he seems so serious.

"Yes, I love you."

"Are we going to try to make this work?"

"Yes."

"Well, part of that is dealing with old boyfriends or girlfriends. I can deal with… The Grinders," says Dan, but the fact he can't even say Truth's name speaks volumes. I smile at him. As long as I don't show Truth any added affection, maybe we'll be all right.

CHAPTER 22

TRUTH

I'm sitting out on the veranda outside my room enjoying a drink when I see Dark Ink meandering up the trail. It's been a while since I've seen them, and I have wanted to talk to Dave about them. They are on their way to becoming superstars, and would make a great opening act for us when we go on tour. I know Kat hasn't given her approval on anything yet, but I like to plan. The Grinders have been out of the public eye for a little while now, and these guys have a whole new generation of fans we can tap into, and we'll be good for them, too.

I stand and hang over the railing and yell, "Hola, Dark Ink! Welcome to Casa Reynolds!" They all look up and wave. "Come on in, the beers are cold, and the food is hot!"

"Hey, Truth!" yells Amy, and she grabs Dan's hand and drags him toward the house. She looks good, and I heard she and Dan are an item. Good for her, she deserves to be happy.

I can hear girly screams, so I'm assuming Kat and Amy are bonding on the front veranda. I throw back the rest of my drink and head downstairs. Kat is a homebody, so I know everyone will be in the kitchen where she'll be trying to ply them with food and drinks.

As I walk into the room, Dave comes toward me and whispers, "Keep away from Amy." Then he turns around and says to the room, "Who wants a drink?"

I hold up my empty glass. "You can fill me up again if you'd like."

He smiles at me, grabs my glass, and heads for the fridge. I look around the room, and everyone has eyes for me except for Amy, who's staring at Kat so intently, it must hurt.

"Hey, guys, how's the album coming along?" I ask.

"Really good, man, we're nearly finished. Hey, if you could spare some time, we'd be grateful if you listened in as we put the final touches on it?" says their lead guitarist. I think his name is Everett.

"I'm sure Truth has better things to do," says Dan with a scowl on his face.

"Yes, I'm sure he does," agrees Dave.

"Well, there's not a lot to do here in terrific Tourmaline, so I'd be happy to help," I reply.

"I'm sure Dark Ink can manage without you. Besides, I have something else I want you to do," says Dave.

I'm confused, these guys haven't hit it big yet, and I've been in this industry for a little while now. Surely, I can offer them some assistance. Kat takes one look at my face and gives a slight shake of her head. She goes across the room to Dave, grabs my drink, and walks it to me.

"Truth, honey, come out on the deck with me for a minute. I have wedding stuff I need to get your opinion on." She turns and looks at the others. "We'll only be a minute, feel free to raid the fridge and the liquor cabinet." A few of them chuckle, and Dave smiles at us as she pulls me toward the back deck.

I walk out and say, "Kat—"

She holds up her finger and shuts the door behind her, then pushes me further away from it.

"What the fuck is going on?" I ask.

"Dan is having an issue with you and Amy. So, to keep the peace, could you please steer clear of her?"

I don't normally get angry, but whatever passes across my face makes Kat take a step back. "Right," I growl sarcastically as I head back toward the door.

"Truth, don't do anything stupid!" she hisses at me.

I open the back door and stalk through the kitchen, running straight into Amy. I grab her by the arms to prevent her from falling and spill my drink everywhere.

"Jesus, Amy, I'm sorry. Are you okay?" I ask.

"Get your hands off her," growls Dan from the opposite side of the room.

I keep my eyes glued to Amy as I slowly release her and say, "You know, Dan, if you have to hold on to something so tight that no one else can touch it, I don't really think it's yours."

Amy gasps, Dave swears, and I hear a struggle. I turn around to see the members of Dark Ink holding Dan back and laugh.

"Fuck you, Truth!" yells Dan.

"Ah, no, Dan, you aren't my type." I smirk.

"Jesus Christ, Truth, get out!" yells Dave as he positions himself in the middle of the room.

"Let the little fucker go."

Kat's eyes bulge out of her head, and Dave stares at me in disbelief. "Are you mad?"

"Dan, I need you to hear this. I like Amy, she's a great girl, but I don't fuck around with taken women, married or otherwise. Not. My. Scene." He relaxes, and they loosen their hold on him. "I'm going to give you some advice. You're fucking this up. Not only Amy, but for the band as well. So, grow the fuck up." I turn around, and Amy scuttles out of my way as I head for the front door.

When I hit the front veranda, I see a group of brothers about to leave. "Yo! Can one of you give me a lift into town?"

One of them laughs and says, "Yeah, man, but I have NFNF on my bike. Sorry, I don't do men."

"What if I buy you a beer or lunch or whatever the fuck you want? But I need to get out of here."

He nods and says, "Get on, man, I love to hear you play."

"Cool, I'll write you a fucking song. Is that good enough?"

The brothers all chuckle as I climb on, and we waste no time in leaving and heading for town.

When we hit Main Street, I motion for him to pull over. I get off and slap him on the shoulder. He does a chin lift and is gone in a cloud of smoke and burning rubber.

I have on a pair of sunglasses, but with my tattoos and long dark hair, I might as well have a neon sign above my head flashing my name. I do a quick look around and see a group of teenage girls descending upon me. I turn to walk in the opposite direction and run smack bang into Rosie, knocking everything out of her arms.

"Today isn't my fucking day!" I say as I bend over to help her pick up her items.

"Excuse me?"

"Sorry, Rosie. Just having a day. Are you hurt?"

Her face has gone a lovely shade of red as she stares at me. "I'm fine. What are you—"

"Oh my god, it *is* Truth!" screams one of my adoring fans.

I wince, and Rosie grabs my hand and pulls me toward a beat-up yellow mustang.

"Get in!" she orders.

There's nothing worse than having a group of women in a frenzy trying to rip your clothes off. Yeah, it sounds fun, but it's not. They grope you in all the wrong places and way too hard. I don't mind having my clothes ripped off in the privacy of my bedroom, and even a little rough play is nice if I have a safe word, but on the street with more than half a dozen? No, thank you.

Slamming the passenger door closed, I reach over and throw open the driver's door. Rosie throws all of her parcels at me and gets into the driver's seat. She buckles up, starts the car, and floors it, only to stop a short distance from where she picked me up.

"Do up your seat belt," she orders.

"Rosie, we need to go!"

"Do up your seat belt, and we will." She raises

one eyebrow at me, and I fumble for my seat belt, clicking it in place as quickly as I can.

As soon as I'm buckled up, she floors it again, and we leave Main Street at breakneck speed. I study her as she drives. Her brow is creased, and she's got her lips pressed into a straight line. Her skin is a lovely shade of ivory with very few freckles. I've always liked Rosie, but she's normally too timid to speak to me. There's something about her bubbly personality that draws me in. We drive in silence for fifteen minutes when she pulls the car over and stops.

"Do you ever wear your hair down?" I ask.

"When I'm not working."

"Fuck, were you on your way to work?"

"Yeah, Howie is going to be pissed."

"I'm sorry, do you have a phone?" She shakes her head. "Drive me back into town then, and I'll call someone from there. I'm sure there's a bodyguard dying to get out of the boonies and into town."

"Nah, I haven't had a day off in two weeks. If I don't come in, they'll call someone else." Her focus is on something through the windshield, like she's avoiding my gaze.

"Really? I thought you were the only waitress there."

Her face goes red again, and she stammers, "Well... I am, but there's another girl we call if it gets too busy." Opening her door, she gets out, then bends back down to look at me through the open door. "Well, come on!"

I give her a quizzical look, then open my door. We're parked on an old bridge over the river with condemned signs clearly posted.

"Ah, Rosie, is this safe?"

She chuckles at me. "So long as I don't drive across it, we're fine. This used to be the road to Pearl County, but the cost to upkeep the bridge got too much, so they moved the road further down. The kids in town come here to make out..."

My laughter fills the air, and I tuck a piece of her hair behind her ear. "Is that right?" I lean into her, and she backs away from me and falls flat on her ass. "Rosie, I'm so sorry! Are you okay?" I hold out my hands to help her to her feet.

"Yep, only my pride." She dusts off the back of her skirt and moves away from me.

Silence once again fills the air, and I'm inwardly cursing myself for moving too quickly with her. She might be a fan, but she's a small-town girl—a good girl. I've always flirted with her, but we've never really had a conversation.

"Thank you for saving me. Crazy fans can be dangerous. So, do you come out here often?"

"Out here?" She bursts out laughing. "No, I don't. Why are you in town without your bodyguards?"

I'm glad she doesn't come out here with any of the local men. It pleases me, and I smile at her.

"There was a disagreement out at Kat's, and I decided the best place for me was away from there so, I got a lift into town. I wasn't thinking straight, and as normal, it's come back to bite me in the ass."

"What did you fight about?"

"You're assuming it was me who was fighting?"

Rosie's face goes a light shade of red. "Was it?"

I jump up on the railing and sit, dangling my legs over the side. Without thinking, I blurt out, "I had a thing a while ago with Amy, a drummer in one of Dave's other bands. Anyway, her current boyfriend is a dick and told me to keep my hands off her. But that wasn't what pissed me off. It was everyone telling me to leave her alone."

Sliding the sunglasses off my face, I look at her—she looks uncomfortable.

"Are you and her still a thing?"

"Oh, no, no, no, it was a long time ago," I say, trying to reassure her.

"Then why was everyone telling you to keep your hands to yourself?"

"I'm a player and don't do the girlfriend thing, never have. I do have a personal code of conduct, and that's not to mess with another man's woman. I guess my reputation precedes itself, and everyone assumes I'm a man-whore."

"You don't do the girlfriend thing? Ever?" she asks incredulously.

I grin at her. "No, guess I haven't met the right one." Then I wink at her.

"Does that work?"

"Does what work?"

"The smile, the wink, and the line? Do women fall all over themselves for you? 'Cause if they do, it's kind of sad."

"Wow, here I was trying to impress you, and I've come off as sad. This day keeps getting better." I jump off the rail and walk a little further onto the bridge and look down. The river is moving quickly, and the water is clear. It's a beautiful day, warm enough to go for a swim.

"Maybe you already impress me and don't need to keep trying," she whispers.

"Rosie, I'm not the man for you."

"Maybe I'm not looking for a boyfriend. Maybe I'm a woman-whore?"

I look up at her and burst out laughing. "I'm pretty sure it's whore or slut, but not woman-whore."

She chuckles. "Right, slut, I've never been called that before."

"And I rest my case. I'm known internationally for it. You are only, my sweet Rosie, a good girl."

"I could give it a try. I might like it!" she says petulantly.

"Rosie, I have no doubt I could make you scream my name." I move toward her and touch her face.

"Twice even, but where would we be the next day or the day after that?"

She grins at me and pulls my hand from her face. "Arrogant much? Twice even?" She laughs. "Come on, let's get you back into town before you sully my reputation."

Surprisingly, we walk hand in hand back to her car, and I like it. She lets go of my hand, and I wish she hadn't. Opening my door, I slide into her car.

"You need a new car. How old is this thing?"

"It works, I own it, and it saved you from your crazy fans, so be nice to her," she says sternly, but I can see a smile playing on her lips.

"Does *she* have a name?"

"Yes, Daisy."

I chuckle as I say, "Daisy, pleased to meet you. Now, please don't break down on the way back as you're older than both of us put together."

"Daisy is *not* that old, and she works just fine!" She turns the car around, looks at me, and asks, "Where should I take you?"

I grasp her face in my hands and move in to kiss her, but she pulls away and looks down so my lips end up connecting with her forehead.

"Well, that didn't go as well as I thought it would," I say into her bangs.

"Sorry, you're right, though. What would happen tomorrow or the next when you move on? I don't want to live a life of regrets. I think I'd regret it if I were only another notch on your belt," she whispers.

Her words sting me more than they should. I nod and sit back in my seat. I don't blame her, though. "Can you take me to the Savage Angels clubhouse?"

"Sure."

"Want to come in for a drink?"

"No, I don't go into the clubhouse. Those guys are a little too rough for me. Well, one of them was, anyway."

"Did one of them hurt you?" I'm surprised, even though they're a rough bunch, I didn't peg them as the type to hurt women.

"It was at a party a long time ago, and I haven't seen him around town in a while, but I still steer clear just in case."

"Who was it?" I ask.

"His name is Fith, but like I said, I haven't seen him in ages. But a girl can never be too careful."

"You mean the type of girl who picks up a stranger and drives him out to a make-out spot only to turn him down? That type of girl?" I smirk at her, hoping to make her smile.

"You have a point. Thank you for being a gentleman."

"Baby, I'm so far from a gentleman. If only you could read my thoughts and see what I want to do to you!"

She pulls on the handbrake, undoes her seat belt,

and climbs over the seat, so she's straddling me. It completely throws me off guard, but my hands immediately go to her ass and pull her further into my frame. Her hands go to my face, and she lowers her lips to mine. At first, she's gentle, slowly kissing me, then her tongue invades my mouth, and I feel my cock get hard. I grip her hips harder, and she grinds into me.

As quickly as it started, she stops. She climbs back over into the driver's seat, puts on her seat belt, and puts the car in gear.

For a moment, I'm completely confused, then I blurt out, "What the fuck was that?"

"That was me letting you know I'm not as sweet as I look." She has a smug smile on her face, and I'm lost for words. In what feels like no time, she pulls up in front of the clubhouse and says, "You're here!"

"I'm here." I continue to sit in her car and stare at her.

She reaches across me and pushes open the passenger door. "You can get out now."

"Rosie, I'm really confused."

"Don't be, now get out, and you can pick me up tonight at seven. I'll meet you at my work, and you can take me over to Pearl County for a nice dinner. If I were you and I wanted to impress me, I'd book Rangers Steakhouse, okay?"

"We're going on a date?"

"Yes, 'cause I *am* the girlfriend type, you're right. So, you are going to give this a shot. You'll be gone in a week, anyway. It'll be good for you."

"You're going to be my girlfriend for a week?"

"Yep, and you're going to dance with me at Kat's wedding."

"Rosie, have you lost your mind?"

She smiles at me. "Yeah, probably, and before I forget, we're exclusive for this week, okay? Now, get out, I have to get to work."

I stumble out of the car, absently shut the door, and watch her drive away. Dane comes up and stands beside me. I don't notice he's there, as I'm still watching Rosie's car until he slaps me on the back.

"Truth, are you all right?"

"She's weird."

"Rosie?" he questions.

"Yeah, Rosie is weird." I have no idea how I'm supposed to handle this situation.

"She's always seemed very nice to me, and she makes wonderful coffee. Is she a crazy fan?"

"No, I think she's just crazy, and I think I really like it."

He whistles through his teeth and rocks back on his feet. "Well, I never thought I'd see the day when you admitted to liking someone."

"I'm taking her on a date tonight. There's a restaurant in Pearl called Rangers, and I'm taking her there… I don't have a car, so can I borrow yours?"

"Sure, man, but that fucking place is always packed, so make sure you book it."

CHAPTER 23

STELLA

Justice Leaverton smiles at me as he explains the seating arrangements for the guests at Kat and Dane's wedding. Kat rang all the people involved and explained I was helping her, and everyone has bent over backward to be nice to me. I've never had that before. Even the Father at the church was nice. I feel like I belong. This entire town has always stared down their noses at me, so it's weird to be treated nicely.

"As you can see, Stella, there's ample room for a dance floor and for everyone to move around easily, especially now we've made use of the park in front of the hall. Now, do you have everything you need?" He has a slow, lazy smile that's always on his face when he's out in public, which I'm sure every female thinks is only for her. His gorgeous face only has eyes for me right now, and I feel a little lost in him. "Stella?"

"Sorry, Mr. Leaverton, yes, I have everything I need. Kat will only need to order another thirteen decorations for the tables and chairs." I tuck my hair behind my ear, push my boobs out a little further, and give him my best smile.

He frowns slightly and takes a step back. "Call me Justice. I have to get to a meeting, but if there's nothing else?" I shake my head at him. "Good. Then I guess I'll see you at the wedding." He flashes his smile, takes two steps away only to turn back, and says, "Remember to vote for your favorite mayor." He smiles again, winks, and disappears down the hallway.

A sigh escapes me as he goes. He really is one good-looking man. The hair on the back of my neck prickles, and I turn around to see Jonas staring at me. There's a look on his face as he stalks toward me, grabs my arm, and drags me into an alcove, away from prying eyes. There are only a handful of people around, and they don't notice us.

Jonas is six foot six, and he's also deadly when he needs to be, and right now, I feel like prey.

"Jonas, what the fuck?"

"Yeah, Stella, what the fuck?" He pushes me up against the wall and puts his hands on either side of my head. "Why are you helping Kat? Why are you suddenly being so fucking helpful?" he says with a sneer.

"She's marrying Dane, that's why! How long do you think he's going to keep me around if I don't get on his old lady's good side?" I snarl at him.

He's nodding and staring up at the ceiling with a frown on his face. In the distance, I can see Adelynn Turner walking toward us, so I reach up and touch his face. He jerks his head back, but doesn't move away from me. "Don't touch me, Stella, and I'm not buying it. You've had ample time to make Kat your friend. They've been engaged for months, and now you try to make nice? Tell me the truth."

Adelynn is bearing down on us and is only a few steps away. I reach up and put a hand on his chest and one on his shoulder. This time he doesn't move away but growls and puts his face an inch from mine, his eyes are full of rage.

"Jonas, don't be like this. We've had a lot of good times, remember?" I say innocently, with a hint of seductiveness.

"What the fuck are you on about?"

"That's what I'd like to know," says a very pissed-off Adelynn.

Jonas moves away from me so fast he nearly trips, and his precious Adelynn crosses her arms and looks at him with an icy stare.

"Love, it's not what it looks like."

I snort, fixing my hair and top. "Yeah, that's what

they all say." I smile sweetly at her.

She uncrosses her arms and fixes me with the same look she gave Jonas. "With you, I'm sure they all say *that*. Do you ever get sick of being the town slut?"

It's not the first time someone has called me that. I snicker at her and thrust out my boobs. "Listen, sweetheart, if the women in this town looked after their men better, they wouldn't come looking for *me*."

Jonas' reaction wasn't something I planned on. He grabs me by the shoulders and shoves me hard up against the wall with enough force, causing me to cry out in pain. "You do not fucking speak to her! Hell, you don't even fucking look at her, got it?" He pushes me again and lets me go, as though I'm something vile and repulsive that he doesn't want to touch.

He turns, grabs Adelynn by her upper arm, and stalks away. She offers little protest as they leave the building. I'm grinning to myself, watching them go and hoping I've driven a wedge between them.

"I thought we were going to play this smart. What are you doing antagonizing that low-life?"

Standing in front of me is an older gentleman with thick-rimmed glasses and a cane. He looks to be in his early sixties.

"Excuse me?"

"I would, but I need you, Stella," he grinds out

through gritted teeth.

Suddenly, I recognize him. It's Gareth. He has gray hair, and his face is all wrinkled. I reach up to touch him, and he jerks back.

"Don't wreck the makeup, sweetheart. Now, let's get back to your place. I've been following you all morning. Busy little minx, aren't you? Get walking and don't turn around to stare at me, just keep moving."

He motions for me to walk ahead of him as he hobbles on his cane toward the exit. No one would recognize him, not even his mother.

Since Gareth has been staying with me, he's made me clean up the place. It doesn't look fantastic, but it's better now. I normally spend most of my day at the Savage Angels' compound with the brothers, so there was never a need to keep it clean, since none of them ever came here. The dishes are done, my kitchen table is tidy, and I have the same man in my bed. My path to self-fulfillment is really coming along great!

I press the button on the kettle for it to boil and get two cups out of the cupboard. Gareth has been spoiling me with presents since he moved in. He's purchased a new dinner set and cutlery, even the coffee is some fancy European blend he claims is *the best*, but it doesn't taste any different to me. I'd be happy with my usual brand. He walks through the door, pulls off his wig, and leans the cane up against the wall. I place his coffee on the dining table and take a seat, clutching my coffee in my hands. His fingers massage my shoulders, and I close my eyes. It feels amazing. He plays with my hair, twists it into a ponytail, and all at once, the nerve endings in my scalp are screaming as he yanks my hair, forcing me to look up at the ceiling.

A howl escapes me as my eyes fill with tears. "What, baby? What did I do?"

"I saw the way you were behaving with that low-life. You're *supposed* to be gaining their trust, getting into their inner circle. How the fuck are you going to do that if you have one of the major players pissed at you?"

"He thinks he's better than me! You told me not to let people treat me like dirt, and I wanted to show him!" He releases me, and I rub my head and neck. "I don't understand why we're still here! You said we'd leave together and have a life, start a family. Go somewhere warm and wear bikinis and sunbake all day..." My voice trails off as he clutches his sides and laughs at me.

"Wait!" He waves one of his hands at me, still laughing. "You really thought *I* would want to have a family with *you?* Don't get me wrong, Stella, you're a good fuck, and I couldn't have gotten out of the psych ward without your help. I'm grateful for that, but I never said I wanted a family with you." His makeup crinkles up more, and suddenly, he doesn't look so good to me.

Each word is like a stab to my heart. Tears course down my face, and it feels like the air has been sucked out of my lungs. Pushing my chair back, I make my way to the kitchen sink, giving him my back. He's still laughing and muttering to himself about how good he is compared to me. I hear the sound of a chair scraping across the floor and the creak as he sits himself down. My eyes look down, and in the sink is a butcher knife left from last night. He takes a big slurp of his coffee, and my hand moves of its own volition, grasping the hilt of the knife.

"Did you ever care for me, Gareth, or was I only a way for you to get out and come back to Kat?" My voice sounds alien to me, and I can't believe I'm speaking to him like this.

"Kat and I have a special relationship, Stella. You have to know it was always about me and Kat." He continues to laugh.

"What about me? Where do I fit in? Are we even going away together?"

"If I can't take Kat with me, then, yeah, babe, I'll take you with me, but we aren't going to remain a couple. You'll go your way, and I'll go mine."

My emotions are all over the place—hurt and anger are the closest to the surface. "What about my path to self-fulfillment? You said I was on the path."

His evil laughter gets louder. "Yeah, you really

bought into all of that bullshit! Maybe I could become a world speaker and shovel that shit to an audience? *You* seemed to like it."

My vision clouds over, and my heart pounds in my chest. My path to self-fulfillment suddenly becomes *very* clear.

CHAPTER 24

KADE

The whole fucking club is enamored with Kat Saunders. No one even seems to care that the president of the founding chapter isn't even following protocol when it comes to getting hitched. I like Dane, and I covered for him with the rest of the MC regarding the issues with the Abruzzi crime family and the fiasco with one of his men who was running guns out of Tourmaline, but I think he's gone soft.

It was me who moved the gun-running to another chapter, and although he was grateful, he keeps making noises about the MC getting out of illegal activities altogether. He's been buying up real estate and legit businesses, and eventually, they'll pay off, but nothing beats green in your pocket right now.

I'm sitting at the bar in the clubhouse watching him laugh and talk to Truth from The Grinders. Truth looks like a fucking pussy with his long hair and the way he talks. I'm surprised one of the MC hasn't fucking decked him. Dane is lending him his car to take the waitress from Bettie's out tonight. He looks like an MC wanna-be—long hair, tattoos, and a long leather jacket—but he's a little too clean and refined. Dane hands over his keys and walks to the bar, taking the seat beside me.

"Brother, how goes it?" he asks.

"Good, man." I point in Truth's direction. "How the fuck can you stand that pussy?"

He swivels around and stares at Truth. "He takes some getting used to, but I wouldn't cross him if I were you."

I raise an eyebrow and scoff. "Yeah, what's he going to do, hit me with his fucking handbag?"

Dane looks at me. "Try it, go on, I *dare* you to push his buttons. He may act like a pansy, but he knows how to take care of himself. He grew up in a rough neighborhood, and although he avoids altercations, the man can fuck you up if pushed."

I look at Truth again. He's tall, and there's muscle under his long coat, but does he have the killer instinct? I doubt it, and he's a long way from a rough neighborhood now.

Dane interrupts my thoughts about Truth. "Have

you had any further luck with the loft?"

Shaking my head, I throw back my whiskey, enjoying the burn as it goes down my throat. "No. Wherever fucking Fith hid the money, I think it's gone forever, brother."

"No, he said it as if I should know. It was his last breath. Someone has to know where it fucking is."

I agree with him, but I've checked everywhere. Even went to the town planners and got a list of every home with a loft—there weren't many, and none of them knew Fith. Also investigated all the barns in the area and nearly got my ass blown off by more than one farmer who didn't like me poking around his home.

I shrug and motion for the bartender to fill me up. "Need you to go to Marlow and check in on The Cherry. They've had some issues at closing, with douchebags harassing the girls. I normally get Jonas to look after it, but he's wanting to stay a little closer to home these days," says Dane.

Another fucking member of the MC who's become pussy-whipped. Jonas used to be fun to party with, but he's gone soft and gotten himself an instant family.

"Prez, I'm good to go, and some of those women are fine."

"Don't fuck with the merchandise. Those girls work hard, and the last fucking thing they need is to be hit on by us."

"Prez, I do *not* hit on women, but if it's offered, I don't say no." He scowls at me as I throw back my drink. "I'll make sure they get from the club to their cars safely. No one will mess with the strippers."

"Good."

"Dane!" We both turn and look at Truth. "I'm off. Thank you, brother, for the car. Wish me luck!" He does a bow and leaves the building.

Fucking pansy.

"Yeah, he's a real man's man, I can tell by his manly-fucking-goodbye," I say with a shit-eating grin on my face.

Dane shakes his head, he has a smirk on his face. "Like I said, brother, challenge him, but make sure I'm fucking there to see it."

He stands and slaps me on the back, then strides out of the clubhouse. For a big guy, he never makes a lot of noise. I sometimes think he could sneak up on you and break your neck before you even knew what was happening.

"Hey, Reb, you seen my boys?" I ask Rebel, who's playing pool with some of the club's Angels.

"Yeah, Kade, they are over in the garage helping with some of the car services."

I nod at him and head in that direction. Normally, I travel between the chapters, but with one point five million dollars hidden somewhere here in Tourmaline, I've been keeping close. Zeke and JJ are my friends. The MC brought us together, and we're loyal to it, but most of all, we are loyal to one another.

The garage smells of sweat and grease, and both my boys are good with their hands. I see Zeke's ugly boots hanging out from underneath a car, and I lightly kick him.

"Brother, get your ugly ass out here. We're on pussy duty tonight!"

He rolls out, covered in dirt and grime. "Pussy duty?" His eyes flick behind me, and before I can turn, JJ has me in a headlock.

"Get the fuck off me, JJ!" I growl.

He releases me while laughing. "Aww, what, Kade? Did I mess up your hair?"

"JJ, you can fucking stay here, and I'll take Zeke with me to look after the strippers at The Cherry. How does that sound, you cocky little fucker?"

"Aww, brother, don't be so fucking sensitive. We both know you don't want me there 'cause I'm prettier than you, and you'll get no play." He wiggles his eyebrows. *Fucker.*

"You keep telling yourself that, JJ, and one day it might fucking come true." I threaten.

I look down at Zeke, who's grinning at our banter. I hold out my hand, helping him to his feet.

"What time we going?" Zeke asks.

"How soon can you get changed?"

He grins and heads toward the change room where the showers are.

"Tell me I can come, Kade. I'll be fucking good, I promise." JJ sounds like a child in a fucking candy shop.

"Of course, you're fucking coming."

"Why are we looking after the bump-and-grinders?" he asks with a grin and a chuckle.

"Apparently, they are being harassed when they go to their cars after shift. We're playing bodyguard for the evening, beats servicing cars and a lot cleaner, too."

"Brother, you obviously aren't doing it right if it's cleaner." He continues to laugh.

The women who work at The Cherry are premium pieces of ass. They also have regular check-ups with the local doctor, so I know they're clean. The Angels that hang around the compound aren't much to look at. There's one, her name is Sharon, but for some reason, only known to the gods, she's latched onto Bear. He's the MC's Road Captain, and he's not what you'd call a small man. I've tried more than once to get into her pants, but she only has eyes for him. So, the distraction of fine ass is definitely something to look forward to.

Shaking my head at JJ, I head toward the clubhouse. "Come get me when he's all pretty, and we'll go," I say over my shoulder.

CHAPTER 25

ROSIE

My shift at Bettie's finished at five thirty, so I went home and got ready for tonight. Now, I'm sitting at the counter waiting for Truth in a little black dress and my washed hair is down around my face in soft waves. My biggest problem is walking in these heels. They are six inches from hell, but they make my legs look longer than they already are.

"So, Rosie, you haven't told me who your big date is with?" asks Howie. He's like the older brother I never had and looks out for me.

"Truth," I answer.

A woman over in one of the booths spits her coffee on the table, and we both look at her.

"I'm so sorry, but did you say Truth? As in The Grinders?" she questions.

I shyly smile at her.

"Well, aren't we going up in the world then?" says Howie, drawing my attention back to him. "You need me to come along to chaperone? He has a reputation."

I giggle at him. "No, I think I can handle him. Besides, he's really a gentleman."

The woman in the booth bursts out laughing, and I give Howie a quizzical look.

"Ma'am, we close in about an hour, and the kitchen is closing in half an hour. Do you want to order something?" says Howie, staring straight at the woman.

"Could I have a cheeseburger and fries, please? And good luck with your *gentleman*, sweetie."

"I'm sorry, do I know you?" She shakes her head. "Ahh, you must be a fan?"

"No, I'm a little more than a fan. Truth and I are… friends," she drawls the last word out, making me wonder what type of friends.

"I'm Rosie, I work here. You must be here for the wedding?"

"I'm Amy, and yeah, we're all here for the wedding." She sits back and draws one of her legs up onto the seat, studying me.

This has to be the same Amy that Truth had a relationship with some time ago. I'm not sure what to say to her, but I'm saved when Truth opens the door.

CHAPTER 26

TRUTH

I open the door with as much flourish as I can and sitting at the counter is Rosie. She looks beautiful, her hair is down, and she's wearing a little black dress, showing off her gorgeous legs.

"Well, well, well, don't you look simply stunning!" I bow as low as I can and hold out my hand. "Your chariot awaits, my lady!"

She giggles and hops down off the seat. Out of the corner of my eye, I can see someone else sitting in a booth, and they clap. I flick my eyes toward them and see Amy lounging there. Without even thinking about it, I immediately stand up straight.

"Oh no, don't let me stop you from wooing the local waitress. Rosie, isn't it?" she says, her voice dripping with sarcasm.

"Hello, adorable Amy. What brings you into Tourmaline? Thought you'd be with the boyfriend, licking his wounds." Rosie stops advancing toward me and looks a little confused.

I close the gap between us and grab Rosie's hand, running my thumb across her knuckles. She gives me a tentative smile, but there's fire lurking behind her eyes.

"Needed some space. If I'd known you were coming in, we could've come together."

"Kind of hard when we aren't staying in the same place, but yes, you could have called," I reply to her.

Howie walks out from the kitchen and places a burger and fries in front of Amy.

"Well, angelic Amy, enjoy your meal. Now…" I lean into Rosie, "… let's go find ourselves something to eat!"

"You could order here? The food's supposed to be good," says Amy.

"The food here *is* good, but I have it on good authority if you want to impress someone on a date, you take them to the Rangers Steakhouse in Pearl. That's where we're going," I say, grinning at Rosie, who goes a lovely shade of red.

"You? On a date?" scoffs Amy.

I glance at her, then give Rosie my full attention. "Yes, it's where one takes their girlfriend, so yes, a date."

"Girlfriend?" Now she's really annoying me. Her

laughter fills the room, and Rosie bites on her bottom lip, and her gaze falls to the floor.

I grab her chin and tilt her head back. "Yeah, my girlfriend. You should know what that is. You are, after all, *Dan's* girlfriend." I pin Amy with a look. "Or have you forgotten?"

Her eyes bulge out of her head, and I tug Rosie toward the door, but she won't move. I give her an inquiring look.

"Truth, I'd like you to meet Howie." She looks at the young cook. "And Howie, this is Truth."

Howie holds out his hand, and I let Rosie go to shake it. His grip is a little too strong, and he squares his shoulders.

"Nice to *formally* meet you, Truth." His eyes flick to Rosie.

"Absolutely, honorable Howie, a pleasure!"

"Our Rosie is special. Make sure you treat her right," he says firmly.

"Howie!" Rosie giggles.

My eyes lock onto Rosie's. "Yes, my man, I absolutely know how special she is."

With that, I grab her hand and start moving back toward the door.

CHAPTER 27

AMY

If I hadn't seen it myself, I'd never have believed it. Truth is going on a date, and he's completely enthralled with her. I watch as he makes a big deal of opening the door to the café and helping her into the car. Then, he runs around to the driver's side.

I mutter out loud, "Oh my God."

The cook, Howie, is also watching them leave. "Did you say something?"

"I can't believe it. I didn't think he dated, let alone have a girlfriend. How long has it been going on?" I ask, with bewilderment.

"He's been coming in here ever since Kat Saunders moved to Tourmaline. Rosie saved him from a group of girls earlier today. He's always been nice to her. But this is their first date, so it's very new... as in today new, I guess?" says a confused-looking Howie.

"Only today?" He nods. "Well, good luck to her." I know I sound bitter, and I have no idea why.

"You need anything else, just yell. I'll be in back cleaning up."

I absentmindedly acknowledge him and put a fry in my mouth. I eat it without really tasting it as I ponder why I'm upset over Truth and another woman. After all, I *do* have Dan, and he can be incredibly sweet. Although, I don't think we've ever been on a date. *Maybe that's why I'm so jealous?* I pick up the burger and take a huge bite, dripping sauce down my chin. It's only a cheeseburger, but the flavor is good.

My phone buzzes, and I look down at the screen. Dan has sent me a selfie of him and the guys all drinking a beer. He has a goofy look on his face, and I realize I really don't care who Truth is seeing. Dan is a good guy, and he cares for me.

I take another bite of the burger and hold up my phone and take a selfie, with the caption, *'Wish You Were Here'* and hit send.

He sends back a love heart with *'Come Home.'*

"Hey, Howie!" I yell.

He pokes his head out from the kitchen. "Yes?"

"I need to settle up, and could I get these fries to go?"

"Sure can."

I give him my best smile and finish my burger. Truth may be a good fuck, but nothing beats having a relationship with someone who cares about you.

CHAPTER 28

KADE

We ride three abreast until we hit Marlow, the closest big town to Tourmaline. Night has descended on the city, and we head straight to the club. It's in a fairly good part of town, but with this type of business, it can attract the low-lifes.

Parking side by side at the front of the club, we dismount, and one of the bouncers on the door approaches.

"Hey, Kade, JJ, Zeke. Dane told us you'd be coming."

I nod at him. "Yeah, man, babysitting duties."

"The girls will be happy to see you. I know the MC doesn't come here often, but your presence may be all we need to keep the perverts away."

"Yeah, is the manager here?"

"Tobias? He's in his office at the back."

"Thanks, man."

The boys follow behind as I walk into The Cherry. Stepping past the bar, the stage area, the girls change rooms, we find Tobias sitting behind a desk on the phone in his office. He motions for us to come in and sit down. I look at the guys, and Zeke shrugs and sits, JJ does the same.

I study Tobias as he talks on the phone. He's a fairly big guy, kind of flashy with silver rings on every finger. He has tattoos down both arms, and I'm wondering why he isn't in the MC.

There's a shelf in his office, high up on the wall opposite the desk, filled with small figurines. I pick one up, and it's a small crystal cat. These aren't the sort of thing I'd expect to find in a strip club.

"The girls give them to me," booms a deep voice from behind me.

I place it back on the shelf and smirk. "They're interesting."

"It started as a joke, and now, whenever I have a birthday, or Christmas, or one of them thinks I'll get a kick out of it, they leave them on my desk. As you can see, I have so many, I put a shelf up."

He stands. He's easily six foot seven. His hair is pulled back in one of those man buns, and he's wearing a black t-shirt with a gold cross around his neck.

He holds out his hand to me. "Tobias Dupont, you

must be Kade?" I nod at him, and we shake. "Cool, the girls will feel better with you in the house."

"Tobias, have to ask, man, why aren't you handling this yourself? You look more than capable."

He frowns and squares his shoulders. "I'm the public face of this establishment, and Dane doesn't want me to get my hands dirty." He looks me up and down. "It doesn't mean I won't, or I haven't, but he'd rather the MC was the muscle here. The bouncers do a fine job, and they are tough motherfuckers, but Dane felt a stronger presence was needed. I thought he'd send Jonas."

"Jonas, like everyone else in the Tourmaline chapter, is pussy-whipped," I say with disgust. JJ and Zeke chuckle from behind Tobias, while the only reaction I get from Tobias is a raised eyebrow.

The door to his office flies open, and a dark-haired woman in an electric-blue satin dressing gown which barely covers her ass storms in.

"Tobias!" She falters as she sees us in the room.

"Yes, Destiny, what's the problem?"

She looks at us, then gives her attention back to Tobias. "You shifted my number to a later time slot. Why?"

"The club is busier then, and we get asked for you. It's good business for you and me."

"I've got a date. You can't just spring this shit on me."

"Ah, sweetheart, tell your *date* to pick you up later. I'm sure he won't mind waiting, probably used to it." I chuckle at her.

To my surprise, she puts both hands on her hips, cocks out a hip, and pins me with a stony stare. "Well, *sweetheart*, he has no idea I do this for a living, and I met him at school. Not everyone who's in this business is a whore. Just like I'm sure not everyone in the MC is a low-life, illiterate asshole looking for a free lay in a strip club."

JJ and Zeke laugh, and Tobias grabs her shoulders. "Calm down, Destiny. Can't you ring him and make it for another time?"

She sighs and flicks a piece of hair out of her face. "Yes, I can, but it's not the point. It's not like I wasn't here last night, and you could've mentioned it then. All I ask for is a roster I can stick to, not one that's changed at the drop of a hat."

"Don't you mean g-string?" I chuckle.

"Oh, he thinks he's funny," she says to Tobias, then turns her glaring eyes at me again. "Go back to your MC, we don't need arrogant assholes like you," she sneers at me, then turns on her heels and storms back out the door.

"Are they all as feisty as that one?" I ask, staring at the empty doorway.

"Destiny is our number one act. More men and some women come here to see her than any of the other girls. Treating her like a whore will not win you any favors, and she's not one. She's too fucking smart for her own good. She's studying to become a lawyer. She has a brother on death row, and she's convinced he didn't do it. Destiny has a good heart, and she only does this to pay the bills."

He follows her out the door, and JJ says, "Well handled. I can see us all getting laid by the end of the night. How about you, Zeke?"

Zeke swipes him across the back of the head. "Smartass." He stands and walks out of the room.

"Was it something I said?" asks JJ as he rubs the back of his head, chuckling.

"No, brother, I'm thinking it was something *I* said," I reply.

We go toward the front of the club, and I see Zeke at the bar, talking to the barmaid. Holding up my hand, I indicate I want a drink as JJ and I sit at a table in the corner. We still have a good view of the stage, but we aren't taking up any of the premium tables.

A waitress places a drink down in front of each of us. "Compliments of the house," she says while giving a wink and goes back to the bar. I do a thumbs up to Zeke, who doesn't notice, as he's deep in conversation with the barmaid.

"Looks like someone has already picked his girl for tonight. What about you, JJ?" JJ is five foot nine and all muscle. He's particular about the women he sleeps with. They always look the same—blonde, blue-eyed, all-American good-girl-looking types.

He surveys the room. "Nothing grabbing me yet, but the night is young."

I grin at him, take a sip of my whiskey, and check out the talent on stage. She has long brown hair and is twisting up and down on a pole. Her tits are obviously fake, but they still look good, and I'm looking forward to seeing her take her top off.

The beat of the music picks up, and she gyrates across the stage. Men stand up and place bills in her g-string while their buddies slap them on the back. It's not a bad-looking club. I've certainly been in worse. It's decked out in reds and blacks while the floor is polished concrete and really easy to keep clean. Nothing worse than carpet that smells like vomit and alcohol.

JJ taps my arm and points toward the front door. Standing at the entrance are two members of the Minions of Death MC. They enter the club and sit at a table near the stage, then two more walk in, and one of them heads for the bar and stands next to Zeke. Zeke looks him up and down, and the guy does a chin lift. We've never had any trouble with the Minions before, and they occasionally help us out, but to my knowledge, they don't normally frequent our clubs.

Tobias walks up to their table, slaps a few backs, and it's smiles all around. He motions to us in the corner, and one of them gets up, then he and Tobias make their way to us.

I quickly glance at JJ, who gives a slight nod, indicating he has his Glock out and is resting it on his leg under the table.

He shrugs at me. "Better to be safe than sorry, brother." I smirk and stand when they reach the table.

The Minion holds out his hand, and Tobias says, "Kade, this is Lockie, he and his boys are here to see Destiny."

I shake his hand. "Destiny? You like hell-cats?"

"Yeah, I do. She's a fine-looking woman, and I'm not going to lie to you, Kade, we own the Pink Pussy on the other side of town, and she's stealing business. We came over to see what all the fuss was about."

"It's cool. Don't steal her, and we'll be good."

"Minions come in from time to time, but they know the rules," interjects Tobias.

Lockie heads back to his boys, and I look at Tobias questioningly. "What? They drink up big, and they treat the girls right. None of the girls who work here would go across town to the Pink Pussy, it's nasty compared to here."

"Does Dane know?" JJ asks.

"Never had cause to tell him. They behave, they look, and don't touch. At the Pink Pussy, you pay enough, and you can touch all you like."

"The girls don't do private lap dances?" Surprise

is in JJ's voice.

"Didn't say that." He winks and walks over to the bar.

JJ shoots me a grin, and I sit back down. It's going to be a long night, and the Minions of Death had better be on their best behavior.

The noise of the club becomes annoying, and the fake smoke machine is giving me a headache. I go to the men's room, and then walk to the back of the club and out the back door to clear my head. Standing out there in her blue robe is Destiny, hunched over, and I hear her hiccupping.

"What's up? Boyfriend find out you're a stripper?"

"Fuck off." She dabs her eyes with a tissue.

"Whoa! We're already at the fuck off stage? Shit, I didn't even get to tell you my name."

"Like I care. Please leave me alone and go back into the club." She sighs and leans up against the back wall of The Cherry.

"Okay, I'm a dick also known as Kade. What's the problem?"

"Why would *you* care?"

"I don't, but you're apparently *the* stripper here. So, in the interests of business, share with someone who doesn't give a fuck. I can offer an unbiased opinion." She scowls at me, her makeup is really heavy, and I blurt out, "Why do you wear so much fucking makeup? You don't need it."

Surprise washes across her features. "It's the lights when you're on stage. If it's not heavy, I look washed out."

"Guys are looking at your face?"

"Funny and fuck you." She turns her back to me and walks a little further away.

"Well, at least you aren't crying anymore."

Without looking at me, she asks, "When is Jonas coming back?"

"I don't think he is. He's gone and found himself a permanent fuck with some chick in Tourmaline."

She twirls back around. "Is it Adelynn?"

"No fucking idea, she works at The Country Inn."

She raises both hands above her head and does a fist pump. "Yay! It *is* Adelynn. He's had it bad for her forever. I'm so glad he finally worked it out."

I smile at her. "You and Jonas swap war stories?" She nods. "So, why were you so upset before?"

"My date wasn't very understanding about me canceling. Apparently, he knows what I do for a living, which means so does everyone else at school. I was a dare, a bet," she says bitterly.

"Sounds like a prince. Fuck 'em. You do what you

have to do to get by. What you do for a job doesn't define who you are. It's all on the inside."

Her face softens at my words, and I think with all the makeup off, she'd be pretty.

"Do you give private lap dances?"

She wrenches open the door. "Fuck you, Kade." Then she slams it hard, leaving me alone in the alley.

A bouncer appears from the shadows. "That was not cool, man. She's a nice girl."

"I wasn't asking for a lap dance. I was asking if she did them. It's two different things."

"The answer is no. She gets asked all the time, but Destiny doesn't even let the guys touch her. She places a hat down at the end of her dance, and they put their money in it. It's a job, a way to pay the bills, but she's no whore." He stares at me a moment longer, then melts back into the shadows.

Taking a deep breath, I head back inside. The lights have dimmed, and the DJ is introducing Destiny to the crowd. I rejoin JJ and Zeke at our table in the corner and a waitress comes over with three waters, and I thank her.

"Is there a problem? Why are we drinking water and not something harder?"

"The Minions are getting rowdy. Tobias says it's nothing to worry about, but I'd rather be ready than swinging slow 'cause I'm wasted," replies Zeke.

I glance over at the Minions, and they look like

they are having a good time. The lights go out, and a spotlight shines on stage. At first, it looks like nothing's happening, then my eye catches movement in the corner. Destiny's head peeks up over some black feather fans, and with her black hair, her face stands out, and I focus on it. Now I understand why she wears so much makeup. The lights slowly come back up, and a softer spotlight hits her from behind as she sashays all over the stage. Occasionally, she drops one of the fans exposing more skin, but she still has on her costume, so not much skin is revealed. The beat picks up, and she smiles suggestively at the audience, and I look around the room—everyone is watching her. Some have their drinks halfway to their mouths, frozen in time. Fluidly, she undoes her dress and turns around to show us her back with its creamy ivory skin. I've leaned forward to see better, and half the room does the same.

She's lost in the music, and her dance is a work of art. The dress drops to the floor, but those damned fans keep her covered. She smiles seductively, and her G-string is kicked from her high-heeled shoe. I watch as it flies in the air, and two men try to grab it, then argue over which one it belongs to. One of the bouncers taps one on the shoulder, and they immediately stop. The one with the G-string smells it and puts it in his pocket, smiling in satisfaction.

My attention is drawn back to the stage, and the soft back light has become brighter, allowing us to see her naked silhouette behind the fans. The song ends, and she's at the back of the stage. She places both fans in front of her, turns, and shows us her naked body from behind for an instant, then disappears as the curtain falls.

I didn't even see her place a hat on the stage, but I can see men and a few women putting money in it. One bouncer keeps an eye on it, and when they're done, he removes the hat. I'm halfway across the club when a hand rests on my shoulder.

"She's good, isn't she?" It's Tobias, and he looks serious.

"Yeah, man, better than good."

"She'll be needing you to walk her to her car. Destiny only has one show, and it's changed weekly. She doesn't stay around after, and they keep coming back for more. Make sure she gets safely to her car." He walks away without a backward glance, and I go in search of Destiny.

When I arrive at the changing room door, it flies open, and Destiny walks straight into me. My hands go to her shoulders to steady her. Her skin feels soft and warm under my hands, and I feel my cock tighten against my jeans.

"Hey! What's the rush?"

"The Minions of Death are here, and I do *not* need another run-in with Lockie telling me I need to work for him."

"That happen often?"

"Only when they are losing business, and they blame me." She looks around my frame and then up at me. "I need to go."

"Come on, I'm the designated babysitter to get you safely to your car."

"You?" She looks at me in disbelief.

"Yeah, me. Let's move." I'm not sure why I am upset with her lack of enthusiasm. She heads for the back of the club, and I grab her arm, stopping her. "Why are you going out the back?"

"My car is parked at the end of the alley for a quick getaway."

"It's also dark out there and easy to hide." I remember the bouncer who hid in the shadows.

"If I go through the front, I have to play nice with the customers. I'm not in the mood tonight, or any night, for that matter. It's a sixty-foot walk to my car." She looks at my hand on her arm. "Please don't make me go out the front doors."

I let her go and point toward the back door. "Come on." When she gets to the door, I stop her. "Let me go first."

I open the door and come face to face with a small man holding a bouquet of pink flowers. His eyes widen at the sight of me, and he backs up.

"You looking for someone?" I growl.

Destiny looks around me and pushes me to the side. "Hello, Harold, we've talked about this. You can't be out here. It scares the girls. Now scoot."

"You were magnificent tonight, Destiny." He thrusts the flowers out in front of himself in her direction. "I got your favorite color. I remembered."

She purses her lips together and smiles. I reach out and take the flowers from him. He scuttles further back down the alley. I hold them up, inspect them, and hand them to Destiny.

"Harold, you'll *not* do this again. Do you know who and what I am?" His head bobs up and down, and he reminds me of a scared animal. "Good. I *never* want to see you out here again, you got that?" His head continues to move, and he looks like he's going to piss himself.

I grab Destiny's arm and move her away from him.

"Harold is harmless."

"Harold may look harmless, but you can never be too sure. No need to put yourself in a fucking dangerous situation if you don't have to."

We make it to the end of the alley, and she stops us to get her keys out of her bag.

I sigh at her.

"What?" She looks over her shoulder at me.

"Your keys should already be in your hand. What if we got to the end of the alley and someone was waiting for you? Your keys don't only unlock your car, they can also be used as a weapon to defend yourself."

She huffs at me and pushes the button to unlock her car. It's a green, beaten-up piece of shit.

"*That's* your car? How much do you get paid? 'Cause whatever it is, it's not enough."

"Oh, shut it. It works, it gets me from A to B, and that's all that matters."

Opening her door, it makes a huge metallic screech, and I grimace at the sound.

"How old is this thing?"

"It's only fifteen years old, she's had a hard life, but I'm taking care of her now," she says affectionately, running her hand across the top of the roof of the car.

I laugh at her as she climbs into it. The interior looks okay, but the outside looks like every panel has met with some kind of blunt-force trauma. "Destiny, do you need me to follow you home? Will it even start?"

She turns the ignition, and to my surprise, it works first try.

"See, she loves me."

"When are you back here again?"

"I'm not on for three days. The club is closed down for Dane's bachelor party, and I have two days off owed to me. Which is good, as I'm behind in my studies."

I shut her door, and she winds down the

window. "Are you going to his party, right?" I ask.

"Oh, no, you're all a little too wild for me. I have school the day after, anyway." She frowns and puts the car in drive.

"You going to be okay at school?"

"I'm a big girl. See you around, Kade." She winds the window up and takes off.

I watch her car until I see she turns off into a side street. She obviously bewitched me because as I turn around, Lockie is standing on the sidewalk, and I hadn't heard him approach.

"She'd make a fine addition to my stable of girls." He leers.

"It's her choice, but I don't think Dane would give her up so easily."

"Rumors are your president's gone soft."

I close the gap between us, my fist connects with his jaw, and he buckles and falls to his knees. Out of the darkness, the other three emerge. I steady my stance, waiting for the onslaught.

Lockie gets to his feet and holds up a hand, signaling them to stop moving. "I may have deserved that, boys." He massages his jaw. "That was your only free shot, you get me?"

"You'll remember my club is bigger and stronger than yours. Talk all the shit you want about your president, but mine? Fuck you, Lockie, and everyone with you." I sneer and spit on his boots.

The Minions advance upon me. Lockie swings at

me, but I duck and land a blow to his mid-section. I feel a sense of accomplishment at his grunt of pain. Unfortunately, it's short-lived when the others grab my arms. As I try to get free, Lockie straightens and walks toward me with a predatory gleam in his eyes, and he pummels my face and body. He has a ring on one hand, and I feel my flesh rip whenever he connects to my bare skin. I struggle against those who hold me, and my rage is fueled as he continues his beating.

A loud whistle pierces the air, and for a moment, my captors loosen their hold. I get free and punch Lockie in the face. I hear the crunch as his nose breaks and blood spurts down his chin.

My boys help me, and between the bouncers who join in and us, we teach them a lesson. All my attention is on Lockie, and I have him up against the club wall, hitting him repeatedly. As I take another swing, a hand grasps my arm, preventing me from following through.

With wild eyes, I turn, ready to attack whoever has stopped me. Zeke is there with both hands up. "Kade, it's me! You keep hitting him, you'll kill him, and we don't need a war." I know he's trying to reason with me, but fuck it.

I shake my head to gain some clarity, and JJ says, "Let's get you inside, brother, and see to your wounds. These fuckers are done for the night."

I tentatively touch my face and mutter, "I had it

under fucking control."

Zeke snorts. "Yeah, brother, we could all see that. Four on one, you had it *all* under fucking control."

JJ slaps my back. "Next time, we'll let you do it all yourself, and we'll sit quietly by and do nothing. Until then, let's get you inside."

I nod and give him a bloody smile. "Yeah, brother, I can see you sitting on the sidelines fucking watching," I say sarcastically.

He lightly punches my arm and runs toward The Cherry's back doors. I cock an eyebrow at Zeke, who shrugs. "You know how excited he gets after a fight. He'll be wired for hours."

It's true. JJ thrives on violence and mayhem. If he didn't have us to keep him in line, he'd have ended up in prison, or worse, years ago.

"Go keep an eye on him, I'll be in soon."

Zeke smiles and looks at the Minions on the ground. "See you inside." He kicks one of them on his way past and signals for the club's bodyguards to follow.

When they head for the backdoors, I bend down and pull Lockie's head up. "You awake?"

He opens one eye, barely, but the other is swollen shut. A groan escapes him.

"Keep away from The Cherry and keep away from Destiny. This is our only warning. Next time, there will be blood. Do. You. Get. Me?" With each word, I bounce his head against the wall.

I stand and head back inside. Dane will have to be told about this, and I know he won't be happy.

CHAPTER 29

ROSIE

The drive to the restaurant is done in silence. Truth keeps giving me the odd look, but says nothing to me. By the time we get to our destination, my stomach is full of butterflies. Amy appears to still have some affection for Truth, and he really didn't ask me on a date or to be his girlfriend. I'm sitting here in my six-inch heels feeling like a fool. He's probably only being nice to me. It's not like I gave him an opportunity to say no.

The car stops, and I take in my surroundings. We're in the parking lot of the Rangers Steakhouse. I feel Truth staring at me, so I avoid his gaze and stare at my hands in my lap.

"You know you don't have to do this. We could just go. It's been a long day, and these shoes are killing me. I could really use a good night's sleep."

"Rosie, please look at me." Slowly, I raise my eyes to his, and he's smiling. "Have you eaten?" I shake my head. "Is the food here any good?" I nod. "Let's go eat 'cause I'm starving, and you can leave those shoes in the car. You don't need them."

He opens his door and comes around to my side, opening my door. As I go to step out, he drops to one knee and takes off my shoe.

"Truth! I can't go into a restaurant with no shoes on!"

"Why not?" He looks up at me.

"Because it looks bad," I hiss.

He puts my shoe back on, and holds out his hand. "Come on."

I grasp it, and we walk hand in hand to the restaurant. Once inside, the Maître D guides us to our secluded table at the back of the room and away from prying eyes. I sit down, and Truth motions for the Maître D to leave, and as soon as he does, Truth drops to his knees, again, and takes my shoes off.

"Truth!"

"You said your feet were sore, so this will help." His hands linger on my calf, and he slowly moves them up my body as he stands. When he towers over me, he places a light kiss on my lips, and my breath catches. "Feel better?"

I don't trust my voice, so I smile, and a wolfish grin spreads across his face as though he knows the effect he's having on me. A part of me can't help but wonder how many women he's done this to, and if Amy was one of them. He grabs his chair and positions it next to mine, moving the cutlery over.

"What are you doing?" I ask.

"I'm too far away from you, and I can't touch you from all the way over there." He tilts his head to where he was supposed to sit.

My smile betrays the fact I like that he's done this, and he grins at me. "Do you do this often?" I ask.

"Go out to dinner with a beautiful woman and take off her shoes? No. Never."

I can feel my face burning as he grasps my hand and holds it to his lips. I'm staring into his dark brown eyes, completely lost in the moment when a bright flashing light goes off, and a man yells out questions.

"Truth, who's the woman?"

"How old is she? Little young for you, isn't she?"

"How long have you been seeing her?"

In between his questions, the flash of his camera nearly blinds me. Truth stands and advances on the man when the Maître D grabs him by the scruff of his neck and walks him out. Truth sits back down, anger washing over his features.

"*Fuck*. I'm so sorry, Rosie. You're about to get your fifteen minutes of fame."

"What do you mean?" I ask, confused.

"He works for one of the tabloids, and your picture will be in tomorrow's edition." He runs his hand through his hair and lets out a sigh. "Do you live alone?"

"Yes. I rent a house two blocks back from Main Street."

"You can't stay there alone. I'm sorry, but the crazies will find out where you live. It's no longer safe. You'll have to come and stay with me out at Kat's."

"No, I can't! I'm sure everything will be fine."

"You're right, it will be, but not until I leave town. Kat's house is enormous, so there's plenty of room."

"You're serious?" He nods. "Truth, I know I convinced you to come on this date, and I know Amy is probably more your type. Can't you simply explain it to that man? And that I mean nothing to you?"

His brows draw together, and he tilts his head to the side. "Amy is more my type? Where the fuck did that come from? How can you think you mean nothing to me?"

"She's blonde, pretty, in the same industry, and this *date* was all my idea." I twist my fingers in my lap nervously.

"Okay, let's get something straight. I'm *not* interested in Amy. I *am* interested in you. Yes, you told me to bring you here, but do you really think if I didn't want to be here that I'd have agreed to it?

Rosie, you have to know I like you, have for a while, but I didn't know how to ask you out, wasn't even sure if you'd say yes. It's difficult to meet women who aren't in my industry or affiliated with it in some way. You're different, and you make excellent coffee."

Laughter escapes me. He's thinking of coffee? "I make excellent coffee?"

"Yeah, even Dane thinks so."

I'm not sure if it's nerves, or I'm relieved to know he likes me back, but I can't stop laughing, and after a moment, Truth laughs. He puts his hand on my knee, and my laughter immediately stops, but I'm grinning like a fool.

"Can we start this date from now?" he asks.

"Yes and—"

"Mr.... ahh... Truth, we're so sorry you were harassed by the reporter. Can we get you something to drink? On the house, of course." We look up to see the Maître D standing next to our table.

"I think my beautiful companion would like bubbles, so a bottle of champagne, please."

"Certainly, sir." I briefly watch the Maître D go, and I return my gaze to Truth.

"What's good?" he asks, picking up a menu.

"The steaks here are to die for, and for dessert, you have to try their crème brûlée. It's the best."

His hand returns to my knee, and I feel my pulse

pick up. "Sounds good. But I think I'd rather have *you* for dessert."

Heat pools between my legs, and he squeezes my knee. I'm sure I'm about to burst into flames, but when I glance at him, he looks so self-assured.

"There you go again with your cheap, sad lines. Do I really look *that* easy?"

He sits back in his chair, removing his hand, and I wish he hadn't. A grin plays on his lips. "Rosie, there's nothing easy about you."

"Well, good, glad we got *that* settled." I put my hand on his knee, and he raises his eyebrows at me.

"Ah, Rosie... I, on the other hand, am *that* easy." We both laugh, and I remove my hand, only to have him capture it and kiss my knuckles.

Right at this moment, if we were alone, I know I wouldn't be able to stop him from doing anything he wanted to me. I'm thankful for the room full of people and can't give in to my emotions.

I'm going through my clothes dresser, and Truth is wandering around my bedroom picking up various items, looking at them, then moving on to the next one.

I've thrown clothes and toiletries into a bag, and now I'm standing in my room feeling slightly tipsy, wondering what the hell I'm doing.

"Do you have everything?" I nod at him, and he walks over, grabs my bag in one hand and my hand in the other. "You ever been out to Kat's before?"

"No, I've seen the cottages on the web, though."

"The ones Dane has for rent? Yeah, those are sweet. Wait till you get a look inside his house, it's ten times better. For a biker, he has good taste."

He takes my house keys off me and makes sure my front door is locked, then helps me into the car. The drive out to the house won't take long, and I'm nervous, so I babble.

"Are you sure I have to come out tonight? How about we wait and see? I mean, Kat and Dane have always been very nice to me, but I don't want to intrude. They don't know me, after all."

"Rosie, calm down. I promise everything will be fine. No one will mind you being there." He briefly takes his eyes off the road to look at me.

"Who's staying out there?"

"Me, Dave, our manager, Jamie, Curtis, Blair, Kat, Dane, Emily, and her family."

"Emily and Sal are staying out there?" I inquire.

"You know them? Yeah, they are in one of the cottages with their son."

"Sounds like a full house."

"There will be room for you. Promise."

He pulls into a driveway that goes down to a very large three-story home. Even at night, you can tell it's gorgeous with its wrap-around verandas on every level. Truth parks the car and turns off the engine.

"It's late, Rosie, and everyone will be asleep, so we have to be quiet, yeah?"

"Okay," I whisper.

Grinning at me, he gets out of the car and opens my door. He holds my hand as we walk toward the door. My six-inch heels clack on the cobblestones, echoing into the wilderness. We climb the stairs to the front door, and Truth opens it.

"They don't lock the door?" I whisper.

"No, who would be stupid enough to break in here? Besides, look to your right."

I turn my head, and standing about twelve feet away from me is a member of the Savage Angels MC. I let out a little yelp, and Truth chuckles.

"Evening, Truth, Rosie," says a figure from the dark.

Embarrassed at my outburst, I do a little wave. Truth grabs my hand, does a chin lift, and pulls me inside. I take two steps and cringe as my shoes make what feels like a thunderous noise in a silent house.

He puts my bag down and bends so that his shoulder is at my waist, and lifts me like a sack of potatoes.

"Truth!" I say as loud as I dare.

"Hush, Rosie, you'll wake the house up." I'm hanging upside down over his shoulder, and my hands go to his ass. "Keep doing that, and we might have a problem," he whispers.

He bends, picks up my bag, and carries me up the stairs. All I can see is Truth's leather jacket and the wooden floor as he carries me through the house as though I weigh nothing. Opening a door, he walks in, closes it, then he drops my bag on the bed before taking two steps, and putting me on my feet.

"I could've taken my shoes off!" I hiss at him.

"Yeah, but where's the fun in that?" He winks.

I giggle and look at my surroundings. It's a fairly large room with French doors leading out onto the veranda. He's not moving away from me, and trails his fingers down my arms, linking his fingers through mine.

I look into his eyes, and he raises one of my hands to his lips and kisses my knuckles. My eyes move to his mouth, and he lightly sucks on my hand. My mouth falls open. He lets me go and drops to his knees.

"Sit down, Rosie."

Words fail me, and my knees buckle, but thankfully, the bed is right behind me. He takes off my shoes and sits back on his heels. He takes one of my feet and places it on his thigh and rubs my foot.

"Oh my God, that feels amazing."

He abruptly stands, and I groan in protest. He goes into the bathroom and returns with a bottle, then resumes his position in front of me and pours a liquid into his palms.

"What's that?" I ask.

"Oil. It will make rubbing your feet a little easier on you. Lay back."

With both of my feet on his thighs, I lie back and close my eyes as he massages them. When you're on your feet all day with work, having someone do this to you is heaven. It's been a really long time since anyone has done this for me. At first, I'm only concentrating on Truth's hands on my body, but after a while, I relax and can feel myself becoming sleepy.

"Truth?"

"Shh, close your eyes and relax," he whispers.

"But I'm going to fall asleep."

"It's okay, fall asleep."

"You sure?"

"Shh."

I don't know how much longer I stay awake, but after a bottle of champagne and being spoiled with a foot massage, I drift off.

CHAPTER 30

JASMINE
The Grinders

For the first time since we've been in Kat's house, I beat Truth to the gym. He's fanatical about exercise, as are most of the others. I like to do thirty minutes to an hour on the bike, and sometimes, I play with the weight machines. The guys keep telling me I need to do more strength training, and I will, but I have to ease into it. I prefer jogging or aerobics, not weights.

"If I'd known you were leaving our bed to come exercise, sugar, I could've suggested a different form of exercise."

Leaning against the door, leering at me, is Judge. He's openly admiring me as I ride the bike.

"Funny. I thought you had a busy day today,

something about leaving early, so you could put the finishing touches on the bachelor party?"

"Yeah, but I'd rather put some finishing touches on *you*, sugar."

I giggle. "Well, I have a bachelorette party to get sorted. Of course, it'll be a low-key affair as we aren't allowed to leave this house, but I still intend to get the bride shit-faced."

The smile falls off his face. "Jasmin, Kat is *not* to leave this house. You get that, right? With Gareth Goodman on the loose, a possible arsonist, and a town full of crazy fans, you'd *both* be safer staying here."

He pushes off the door and walks toward me as he speaks. I know he looks after Kat, and he's gone all serious on me, playing the bodyguard.

"Calm down, *sugar*. I know the rules. Dane spelled them out to me perfectly. I do need more bubbles, though, so can you organize that?"

He's slipped back into his easy-going persona. "Sure, how many bottles are we talking?"

"Three dozen. I intend to have a good time." I hop off the bike and walk toward him.

"Thirty-six bottles? How many women are you having out here?"

"Pfft, that's all for me." I link my arms around his neck and stretch up to kiss him.

"Sugar, I know you're a wild woman, but thirty-six bottles are a lot, even for you."

"Yeah, but imagine the drunk sex you can have with me."

A frown creases his forehead. "Ahh, Jasmin, I won't be back out here tonight. I'll be in town with Dane, keeping an eye on things."

"You won't be drinking?" He shakes his head. "Well, that doesn't sound like fun."

"I will see you tomorrow. I'll bring Tylenol and water."

My lips lock with his, and his hands go straight to my ass.

"Get a room, you two." Jamie laughs as he makes his way into the gym.

I unlock our lips and twist my head to look at him while Judge presses his lips to my temple.

"Now, that's the best idea I've heard all morning," I say.

"Well, go, some of us professionals need to stay in top condition so we can perform at our best," Jamie jokes.

"Now, honey, some of us are always in top condition, and I *always* perform at my best on or off the stage."

"Go, be gone with you, woman, and take your boyfriend with you," shouts Jamie.

Judge reaches down, grabs my ass, and I jump up, wrapping my legs around his waist as he carries me down the hall. I feather kisses across his face and down his neck.

"Sugar, I can't play with you right now. Prez needs me in town. I have to go."

"Why'd you pick me up then?"

"Staking a claim is all."

Kissing his neck, I run my tongue up to his ear. "I know the prez. I'm sure it will be fine."

"No, it won't. I have a job to do, sugar, and I'd best go do it."

A sigh escapes my lips as he stops, and I unwrap myself from him. Slowly, he places me on the ground. "Think I'll miss you today."

He raises an eyebrow at me. "You'll miss me? Since when?"

"Since I've gotten used to having you around. I thought maybe we could make this a more permanent thing?" I make it a question, hoping he feels the same way. He's studying me, searching my face for something.

"Sugar, I don't ask what you get up to when I'm not around, but..." he places both hands on his hips, "... since we have been together, no matter how infrequently, I haven't been with another woman. So, for me, Jasmin, this is a permanent thing."

I had no idea he felt this way. He's always played it hard and fast with me. I assumed, like me, he had other 'friends.' I know I need to say something, but all I can do is stare. He reaches out and closes my open mouth.

"It's all good, sugar. I know what a hell-cat you

are. Never expected you to be faithful. It's not the relationship we have, or should I say had?"

"Had... definitely had," I gush out.

His smile widens, and he kisses my forehead. "See you tomorrow, and if your head is still on your shoulders and not in a toilet, we'll talk."

He slowly saunters away, and I watch his ass as he does. The man has a fabulous ass. Someone comes up behind me and wraps me into his frame, only to let go just as quickly.

"Yuck, you're all sweaty. I was going to tease you." I turn around to face Curtis, and he sings, "Jasmin's got a boyfriend! Jasmin's got a boyfriend!"

I swat him across the arm. "Yes, she does. A sexy one at that."

"You smell bad."

"Well, thank you, Curtis. It's called exercise, and how come I'm the only one in the gym this morning? Jamie's only just wandered in. Where's Truth?"

"You haven't heard?"

I shake my head at him. "Heard what?"

"Truth went on a date."

Laughter bubbles up and out of me. "No, no, no. Truth doesn't date, he has sexual hook-ups, but he doesn't date."

"Well, Jas, he does now. Got in late, and I saw him carrying her to his room."

"See, told you, he's found a new fuck buddy."

"You ever seen Truth get dressed up and go out to a restaurant, alone, without bodyguards and all the paparazzi following him?" Curtis quizzes.

"You have a point. I'm going for a shower. Will you make me breakfast?" I ask hopefully.

"No." He frowns at me.

"Aww, come on, Curtis. I'll be nice to you for the rest of our stay." I give him my best smile.

"You're always nice to me. Well, almost always, but I do want something."

"Baby, I have a boyfriend," I smirk.

"Funny. I need you to talk to Kat tonight about getting the band back together. Need you to sell it to her. I need this, Jas, and I think we all need it."

"Could you say need anymore? And could you say, of course, I'll make you breakfast, Jas. Then I might talk to Kat."

In a deadpan voice, he says, "Fine."

I laugh and run up the stairs to shower and change.

On the way as I head downstairs, I pick up my phone, looking at my Twitter feed as I go. This leads me to Facebook, which leads me to Google, which leads me to Truth. Sure enough, there's a picture of him with the waitress from town, but he's kneeling in front of her. It's kind of strange and intimate, but it proves my theory.

I walk into the kitchen without looking up and say, "See, I told you, Curtis, a fuck buddy. The press has captured it perfectly, I think. Actually, it's a weird photo. He's on his knees. Hell, it almost looks like he's—"

"Jasmin! Have you met Rosie?" Curtis practically yells at me from across the room.

My head snaps up, and there, sitting at the kitchen table, is the waitress from town. The same one in the picture on my phone. I put my phone in my pocket and walk over to her, extending my hand.

"No, I haven't. Well, not formally. I'm Jasmin."

She takes my hand and shyly smiles. "Nice to meet you, Jasmin."

Her face is a deep shade of red, and I realize she's wearing one of Truth's t-shirts. It's miles too big for her, and she looks good in it.

"Nice top. I remember that gig. Do you, Curtis?" I turn my head to look at him. "Truth really wanted a t-shirt, and we didn't get one in our dressing rooms. He almost caused a riot when he walked out and stood in line for one." We both laugh at the memory.

"Yeah, the girl who served him was so nervous she sold him a girl's V-neck, so he went back to exchange it. Security was pissed that night." He chuckles.

"You staying for tonight, Rosie?" I ask.

"I think so. Truth said I couldn't go home until after the wedding. He said there are too many crazies in town, and I wouldn't be safe after the press took a photo of me, and I end up all over the internet." She looks down at the table. "I guess you were talking about us when you walked in?"

"No, no, no, ahh… it was a picture of a cat…" My voice trails off as she slowly raises her eyes to mine. I let out a sigh and sit down opposite her. "Rosie, those who love me are used to me putting my foot in my mouth," I say truthfully.

"And she swallows it and looks for the other one," says Curtis with a grin in his voice.

I ignore him and say, "I'm really sorry. We're a family, and we talk about each other all the time, but it's nothing I wouldn't say to his face. Truth is right, though. You shouldn't be home alone. He has some freaky fans who might get upset with you. Curtis and I had a bet a while ago, I won, and he had to cut six inches off his hair. Look how fucking long it is, you couldn't really tell. Anyway, some fans got very upset with me. I had to hire extra security for about three months."

Curtis chuckles. "Don't mess with the hair, Jas."

I shoot him a scathing look and turn my attention back to Rosie.

"Considering you're stuck out here, would you mind helping me with the bachelorette party? I need to decorate the back deck, and my creative flair for that shit sucks."

"I'd love to! Do you have a menu figured out? I could help with that as well," Rosie says with an enormous smile.

"Cool, and no, I don't have a menu sorted out unless you count chocolate penises?" Rosie bursts out laughing, and Curtis places a plate of eggs in front of me. "Aww, thanks, Curtis. I love you."

"Yeah, I bet you say that to all the boys who make you breakfast."

All I do is smile and nod at him as I eat.

"Now, Curtis, we all know she doesn't let them stay overnight. She's more a love-them-and- kick-them-out-before-daybreak type," says Truth as he walks into the room and sits down next to Rosie, placing an arm around her shoulders.

"Funny." I frown at Truth, then turn back to Curtis. "These eggs are good." I shovel in another mouthful.

"Tell me, creative Curtis, who are we going into town with tonight?" asks Truth as he absently plays with a lock of Rosie's hair.

"Dane said he'd organize a car or something. I'm sure Kat will know. Would you two like some eggs? According to Jas, they're good."

"How come I practically had to *beg* you, but for

Truth and Rosie, you'll just do it?" I ask him.

"Because you *always* have an agenda, and Truth is, well, just Truth, and Rosie is cute." We all look at Rosie, who blushes, and Truth pulls her closer to him.

"You keep your eyes to yourself, Curtis, and eggs would be good," replies Truth.

In all the time I've known Truth, I've never known him to be possessive of anyone, and I raise my eyebrows at him. He shakes his head at me and gets up.

"Coffee, I need coffee. Anyone else want a cup?" he asks.

I smirk at him. Rosie says yes, and Curtis passes him his empty mug. I can't wait for the boys to be gone, so I can ask Rosie about the photo and what Truth is like in bed. He doesn't normally let me meet his conquests, so this should be interesting.

CHAPTER 31

JUDGE

I climb off my bike when one of the Angels comes up to me. She's nice enough and seems to have her hooks firmly planted into Bear. She's blonde, blue-eyed, and has a pair of tits you can't help but admire.

"Hey, Judge."

"Hey, sugar, how's it going?"

"Things are going good. I was wondering how many strippers are going to be here tonight?"

"Why, you thinking of trying out?" I ask, and my eyes flick to her tits.

"No, but you know I'm seeing Bear? It's just that..." She looks at the ground and puts her hands on her hips. "I mean, I think it's... well, I—"

"Relax, sugar. Bear only has eyes for you. I know

some of the Angels are going to hang around. You going to?"

"No, Bear told me I have to stay home. MC and strippers only."

I chuckle. "Yeah, that sounds like Bear, and it's probably for the best. Things tend to get a little out of control at these things." I wink at her and head toward the clubhouse.

She grabs my arm and asks, "How out of control?"

"Now, sugar, you've been around us for a while now, so I don't need to spell it out for you. But you needn't worry about Bear, he'll be good." She releases me, and I keep walking, but from the look on her face, she doesn't look convinced.

When I go inside the clubhouse, Bear is just inside the door.

"What was that all about?" he asks, with annoyance in his tone.

It takes me by surprise. Bear is one of the nicest guys in the MC, and normally, nothing gets under his skin. I look back at the Angel and give her a small wave.

She waves back, and I smile at Bear and say, "I was only saying hello, Bear, and telling her I'm available later if she's not busy. She seems pretty interested," I say jokingly.

My gaze returns to his face, and it's flushed with anger. Before I have a chance to tell him I'm messing with him, he tackles me around the waist, pushing me backward, and slams me up against the bar. I'm winded, and the brothers clap and cheer. Everyone thinks it's a bit of fun.

"Sharon belongs to me!" growls Bear as he backs up and slams me into the bar again.

Thankfully, Rebel realizes Bear isn't playing and places a hand on his shoulder. "Ease up, big man. Whatever Judge said to upset you, he didn't mean it. He's *Judge*."

Bear drops me, and my legs buckle as I hit the floor. I'm on my hands and knees, sucking in air.

I'm staring at the floor when Dane's booming voice fills the room. "Bear, *what the fuck* is going on?"

"He was talking to Sharon. He said he made her an offer!" bellows Bear, trying to catch his breath.

Sitting back on my haunches, I look up at him and finally, I speak, "Bear, I was fucking with you. Your woman only has eyes for you. *Fuck*. She was asking me about the strippers. Guess she's worried you'd stray. I told her she had nothing to worry about." I massage my lower back and try to stretch out my battered spine.

"You were fucking with me? But all the Angels like you, *everyone* knows that!" he says with exasperation.

"Well, I guess my super powers don't work on *your* Angel."

He grins at me and holds out a hand to help me to my feet. "Sorry, brother. She's important to me."

"No shit?" I say as I slowly let him help me to my feet. "You nearly broke my fucking back."

Some of the brothers are laughing. I look past them and see a battered Kade and his two entourages walk through the doors. I motion toward them, and the room turns to look.

"What the fuck happened to you?" Dane demands.

"Hey, Prez, we kind of had a run-in with the Minions of Death," replies Kade. His face is bruised, along with a couple of bandages here and there. The other two look fine, except for bruised and scraped knuckles.

"Did you at least give as good as you fucking got?" asks Dane.

Kade nods and heads for the bar. Rebel walks around the counter to the opening of the bar and pours them all a whiskey. I arch an eyebrow at him, and he does one for me too.

I throw mine back in one go and slam the glass on the top of the bar where Rebel refills it. Dane walks up to the bar and signals Rebel for a drink as well. "Start from the beginning, but not until the brothers from the garage are here. Bear, you think you could go get them and cool off at the same time?"

"Yes, Dane," he says, looking sheepish.

We all watch him go, and Dane pins me with a look. "Maybe next time you won't fuck with another man's woman."

"I didn't fuck with his woman, I was fucking with *him*." I stretch and groan as my back clicks into place. "But you have a point. I shouldn't have teased him."

I watch as Dane tries not to laugh, but it rumbles up and out of him, and the brothers who witnessed my assault all join in.

"Fuck you all!" I yell with a smile.

Kade catches my eye and gives me a questioning look. I shrug at him and motion for Rebel to give me another refill.

Dirt, Jonas, and the other brothers from the garage come through the doors to the clubhouse, laughing and shoving each other playfully.

Dirt walks up to me and punches me in the arm. "Heard you got a beating!" he jokes.

Again, the room explodes into laughter, and everyone is having a good time at my expense.

"Yeah, laugh it up, bastards! I'd like to see how you all fare with an angry Bear!" I yell.

More laughter greets me, and I put my hand in the air and give them the finger. All it does is encourage them, and the laughing gets louder.

Dane whistles long and loud, and eventually, everyone quiets down. "The reason you're all here is..."

"To celebrate your last few days as a single-fucking-man!" yells Jonas. "And to see strippers! Where are the strippers?" He looks around the room.

The room erupts into more laughter, clapping, and much whooping. Dane looks down at the floor, and a small smile plays at his lips. He looks up slowly and holds both hands in the air, trying to get us to all quiet down. When this doesn't happen, he points at Kade, and silence slowly fills the clubhouse.

Dirt is the first to speak. "What the fuck happened to you, brother?"

"That's what we need to find out," grinds out Dane.

Kade looks around the room, but his gaze settles on Dane. "The Minions of Death picked a fight, and we ended it."

"Casualties?" Dane asks.

"No, Prez, just hurt egos," Kade responds.

"Any of the girls hurt?" Jonas asks.

Kade shakes his head. "They weren't involved. Seems they think Destiny is stealing their business and wanted to add her to their stable. I suggested you wouldn't like it. They made a disparaging remark, and all hell broke loose."

"What was the remark?" growls Dane.

"That you'd gone soft."

Unexpectedly, Dane laughs, and some of the

brothers join in. "Is it because I'm getting married the fuckers think that?"

Kade shrugs. "Who the fuck knows?"

"Who threw the first punch?" asks Dirt.

"That would be me," replies Kade.

"They were on our turf, talking shit about our prez, and they were four to one," says a fiery Zeke. It's unusual for him or JJ to speak, as they normally let Kade do all the talking for them.

"Where the fuck were you two?" Jonas asks.

"I walked Destiny to her car, and they didn't know. They were still inside when it began." He touches his face and winces.

"Will there be retaliation?" queries Dane.

"I don't think so. I think we worked it out," replies Kade.

"Good." He grins at the three of them. "Get them all a drink for defending my honor!"

Laughter again fills the clubhouse.

"I want to know when the strippers arrive!" bellows Dirt.

The volume goes up considerably as they talk about the strippers, and Rebel lines up a row of glasses on the bar and fills them up with whiskey.

CHAPTER 32

KAT

It's not the bachelorette party I had in mind. We're still at Dane's house, and there's no way in hell he'd let me have it in a nightclub. There's a heavily pregnant Emily, Jasmin who seems intent on drinking everything in sight, Rosie who's acting more like the hired help than a guest, and Adelynn, who's fussing over Emily. But those I love surround me.

"Jas, babe, you need to slow down. Have you eaten anything?" I ask, as I take the glass out of her hand.

"Oh, let your hair down, woman! It's your night!" replies a tipsy Jasmin.

I frown at her. "Anyone else hungry? I know I am."

"I'm always hungry. Let's move this party from the lounge to the kitchen," responds Emily as she struggles to stand.

Adelynn helps her to her feet, and when I arrive in the kitchen, there's a man in there with an apron on and not much else. I stop dead in my tracks, and someone runs into me from behind. Jasmin pokes her head around me and laughs.

I move out of the way, and the others stumble into the room.

"I forgot I organized him! One of the guys must have let him in!" quips an excited Jasmin.

"Ladies, they frisked me, but there's one weapon they missed," he says seductively, and starts undoing his apron.

"No! Don't!" I run toward him and wave my hands at him. "I'm so sorry there's been a miscommunication. We'll not be needing you tonight. How much do we owe you?"

"I've already been paid."

"Yes! He's already been paid, he's ours for four hours." Jasmin winks.

I turn to look at her. "Jas, this isn't something I want. Can we not sit down, have a meal, drink ourselves silly, and it be just us girls and the occasional bodyguard who checks on us?" I plead.

She pouts and looks around the room, but no one offers her any support. "Okay, sorry, big guy, you're out of here. Looks like it's going to be a chicks-only evening." She sounds disappointed.

"Damn! Thought I was going to party with Kat and Jasmin from The Grinders." His smile is intoxicating, but I don't need my man to doubt me in any way.

"Sorry." I point to a bodyguard and gesture for him to come inside.

He opens the door to the deck. "Is there a problem, ma'am?"

"No, there's no problem, but would you mind escorting this gentleman to his car?"

"Absolutely." He stares at the stripper. "No problem at all."

"Have a good night, ladies."

We all watch as he leaves the room, his naked butt out there for all to see. I glance at Rosie, who has gone a deep shade of red, and giggles. Within a matter of seconds, we're all laughing.

"Jas, did you get any food for this event?" I question her.

"Actually, I let Rosie do that. She's the food expert."

Rosie suddenly looks uncomfortable as all eyes go to her.

Adelynn saves us by saying, "Well, if Rosie is in charge of food, I know it's going to be good. What have you got for us?"

Rosie beams at me. "I have homemade pizzas ready to go. They'll take twenty minutes to cook, and I've prepared a cheese platter and crackers for starters followed by buffalo wings and dip."

"I love, love, love buffalo wings, and cheese is as close to heaven as I can get at the moment," enthuses a now-excited Emily. "Although, that man's ass was mighty fine!"

CHAPTER 33

DANE

The strippers have arrived, and as I am the main attraction, I'm sitting in a chair in the middle of the compound. The Angels have hung material and some shit up on the fences, but I can see the press up on ladders clicking away on their cameras.

The strippers who work at The Cherry are a great group of women. They're drinking and partying with us like they do it every day. As I'm drinking tonight, I have asked Judge to keep an eye on them, making sure the brothers don't cross a line.

The music is louder, and "American Woman" blasts out of the speakers. Four of the strippers begin a sexy coordinated dance, each coming closer and removing items of clothing as they do. I'm smiling, clapping, and wolf-whistling. The brothers are calling out my name and making lewd comments about the strippers and me. It's all in good fun, and I'm having a good time, but I have the real deal at home, and it's where I'd rather be.

One of the strippers, I think her name is Amber, straddles my lap and pushes my head between her ample breasts. She smells of sweat and cheap perfume. Amber runs her fake nails over my scalp, and I shudder. The brothers cheer, and she places her lips on mine and forces her tongue into my mouth. I grip her shoulders and push her back. She looks surprised, and for a moment, she stops all movement, then she stands and walks seductively around me. I wipe my mouth on the back of my hand. I've had enough. The music is good, the alcohol is good, partying with the brothers is good, but if I'm going to be kissing or fucking anyone, it will be my woman.

I stand, and all four of the strippers surround me. Thankfully, Jonas can tell I've had enough. He extracts me from their clutches and pushes Rebel into their pack.

The brothers boo and yell.

"Come on, let poor Rebel have some fucking fun! Treat him good, girls!" The brothers soon start cheering Rebel's name, and I go back into the clubhouse to my room. Falling back on my bed, I pull out my phone and dial home.

"Hello!" yells a drunken Jasmin.

"Hey, Jasmin, can I talk to Kat?"

"No! This is our night! Go find yourself some guy friends!" The phone line goes dead.

I lay there looking at my phone when the door to my room throws open. A scantily clad stripper stands in the doorway. I raise up on my elbow and arch an eyebrow at her.

She stumbles into the room, undoing her top as she does. "Hey, Dane," she purrs.

I sit up, scrub a hand over my face and sigh. "Hey, babe."

She throws her top at me. "You don't remember me, do you?" Her words are coming out slurred.

"Sorry, babe, not good with names. Have we met?"

She scrunches her face up, puts her hands on her hips, and thrusts out her naked boobs. "Have we met?" she repeats angrily.

Dammit, a creature from my past. I stare more closely at her. She was once my type—big boobs, trim figure, pleasant face, but no substance. I stand and hand her top back to her, and she throws it across the room.

"My name isn't babe! It's Crystal!" she whines at me.

Keeping my distance from her, I walk over and pick up her top. When I get within arm's reach, I hold out the flimsy material to her.

"Crystal, I'm getting married—"

"Do you know how many guys would *kill* to have me?" She's pacing back and forth, waving her hands in the air. "I'm fucking hot."

She's drunk, pissed, and looking for validation.

G*reat, just fucking great.*

"Crystal, you're hot, and yes, we may have had a thing, but I'm getting fucking married."

"We *may* have had a thing?" she yells.

I look past her. Jonas and Judge are standing in the doorway pissing themselves laughing.

"What?" I growl.

Crystal puts her arm around me and says, "Gotcha! Honey, you're fine, but I'm the only girl here who hasn't fucked you, and the others wouldn't do this as..." she makes inverted commas in the air, "... he's really a nice guy."

"You should see your face, Prez!" says Jonas as he slaps Judge's back.

I look at the woman next to me. She kisses my cheek and puts her top back on. "All's fair in love and war. Have a great night, Dane, and a better wedding."

She pats Jonas on the face as she leaves the room, and they both watch her as she walks away. When they finally look back at me, I've moved toward them and am holding the door.

"You think you're fucking funny?" My voice is flat with no emotion, and the smiles quickly fall off their faces. "Well, you both owe me a fucking beer." I keep my voice flat, but I end it with a smile. "You're a pair of fucking bastards, you know that?"

Relief washes over their features, and they chuckle.

"You were being such a pussy out there with the strippers, we had to do something! Kade's right, you *are* pussy-whipped!" Judge chortles.

"And *you're* not? When was the last time either of you fucked someone who *wasn't* your woman?"

Both look at each other, then it's my turn to laugh with an exasperated huff.

"Maybe we should change the name to Pussy Whipped MC?" Jonas suggests.

"Not. Fucking. Likely. Let's go get drunk and stare at some hot women," I say.

"Now we're fucking talking!" yells Judge.

CHAPTER 34

KADE

I have no idea why I'm here. I have the world's worst headache. Dane's bachelor party went into the wee hours, and instead of sleeping, I'm sitting on my Harley outside the school Destiny goes to, waiting for her to come out.

After Crystal finished messing with Dane, I asked her about Destiny. She told me how Destiny phoned her in tears as the jerk she had a date with the other night embarrassed her in front of her classmates with a lewd comment. She has balls, though, and she didn't let it stop her from going back.

The sun feels good on my face, and I have my head tilted back with sunglasses on. I sigh and let my head fall forward. I see her walking across campus with her hair in pigtails and books in her arms. She looks cute with her hair like that, but when you've seen her almost naked, you know what she's hiding underneath and cute doesn't do her justice.

Climbing off my bike, I discreetly adjust myself as I walk toward her. Her head is down, and she's rushing. I'm a big guy to start with, but as I am wearing my colors, those who get in my path quickly find another route giving me a wide berth.

She walks right up to me, but I don't think she notices me, as her head is still down. Destiny lifts her head slightly, not enough for me to see her face, but enough for her to see my legs in front of her, and she tries to walk around me. I reach out and grab her arm, and she lets out a small squeak.

"Hey, know where I can get a good cup of coffee around here?" It's the only thing I can think of to say, and even to my ears, it sounds lame.

Destiny looks up at me and hisses, "What are you doing here?"

She's looking around to see if anyone is watching, and following her gaze, we have an audience.

Glaring at the onlookers, I turn back and give her my full attention. "Crystal said you were having a hard time. Thought if I showed up in my colors, they might think twice before giving you grief."

Her mouth hangs open, and she splutters, "Why?"

"You're one of our employees, and it's a part of our ongoing duty to make sure you are happy in or out of work." I try to say it with a straight face, but fail miserably.

Her laughter goes straight to my heart, and she links her arm through mine. "Well, if it's part of being an employee, I can't very well say go away. Let's go find you some coffee. You look like hell. Dane's party was a success, I guess?"

"It was a good night. Where are you taking me? Would it be easier to take my bike?"

"No, it's across campus. We can walk. Good coffee and great donuts."

"You eat donuts?" I ask incredulously.

"Donuts are good. Why wouldn't I eat donuts?"

Stopping, I take a step back, our arms unlink, and look her up and down. "You don't look like you *ever* eat anything with fucking sugar."

She laughs again and clutches her books to her chest. "I work out every day, kind of have to if I want to use the pole at work. Seriously, though, why are you here? It's not like we're friends."

I reach out and take her books from her. "I think you've got spunk. It can't be easy coming here when you tried so hard to separate your work life from your... other life..."

Her smile grows, she links her arm with mine again, and we continue our walk. "Crystal told you? I swear, I know better than to share anything with those women, but I needed *someone* to talk to."

We walk in silence the rest of the way to the coffee shop. Opening the door for her, I bow and gesture with my hand that she should go in. Destiny smiles at me, shaking her head, only to freeze in her tracks.

"You're kind of blocking the doorway, so you need to keep walking."

She whirls around and quickly says, "I think we should go somewhere else."

I look at her face, and it's almost panic-stricken. I grab her hand and walk inside, practically dragging her with me. Looking around the room, I see a group of guys sitting in a booth, pointing at her and laughing. Destiny, who looks like she wants to melt into the floorboards.

"Hold your head up high," I demand. She looks up at me, a frown creasing her forehead. "Are you proud of who you are?"

The color drains out of her face, and she gives me a slight nod. "It's just that—"

"Okay, then, fuck them. Where do you want to sit?"

She pulls me away from the jerks in the booth and goes to the other side of the coffee shop.

"This where you want to sit?" I ask, aggressively.

"Kade, please sit down. Don't make a scene. It's hard enough having to deal with them in class with their snide comments, I don't want to deal with them here, too."

I clench my jaw but do as she asks and sit down. Placing her books on the table, I rest my elbows on the tabletop and say nothing.

The waitress comes over and takes our order. I remain silent and stare at Destiny. I'm disappointed she'd let someone make her feel less than.

"What? What do you want me to do, Kade? Walk over there and tell them off? Tell me, tell me what you think I should do!" She's angry, and I prefer it to the meek woman who walked in here.

"I think for some reason, you think they are better than you and Destiny, they aren't. You work hard, and from what Crystal tells me, you study hard. The only opinion in this room that matters is the one you have of yourself."

Her face suffuses with red, and I can't tell if she's going to cry or hit me. Our gazes lock, and neither of us speaks. The waitress comes back with our order and places it on the table.

When she walks away, Destiny breaks eye contact to put sugar into her coffee. "It's not like when I was growing up, I told myself I wanted to be a stripper. I've done the waitressing thing, and it doesn't pay enough to cover the bills. Tobias found me late one night working in a diner and gave me his card, and the rest, as they say, is history."

She's looking at her coffee as she speaks. She seems unable to look me in the eyes, and it pisses me off. She has no makeup on, and with her hair in those pigtails, she looks really young and vulnerable.

I don't respond until she makes eye contact. "You make enough money to pay for your tuition?"

"Almost. I have a small student loan. Nothing like I would've had if I didn't do the job I do."

"Those clowns were giving you a hard time when we came in. Do they have large student loans?"

She sighs. "Well, I guess the ones who don't have a trust fund would."

"So, in the end, *you* will be better off than them as you won't have a huge debt hanging over your head when you're finished?" I ask.

"Probably."

"I've watched you dance. You're good, and you have everyone mesmerized. Although you were naked on stage, we didn't really see anything. I think I saw all of you from behind, but if I blinked, I'd have missed it. My question to you is, why are you letting those fuckers make you feel less than you are? I don't get it." Disappointment is evident in my tone.

"No, I guess you don't." She picks up a donut and walks out of the coffee shop without another word.

I finish my coffee and eat a donut. Then I stand, throw some bills on the table, and walk toward the front door. I have my hand on the door handle when I look over at the dickwads in the booth, and anger washes through me. One of them catches my eye and laughs. It's all I need to head in their direction. Suddenly, they don't look so brave.

"We don't want any trouble." The way some of them talk immediately assaults my ears, but, as usual, there's always one who thinks he can take me. This guy squares his shoulders and sits higher in the booth, trying to stare me down.

"You will not look at Destiny. You will not point at Destiny. You will not laugh at Destiny. If you do, I'm going to come back here with some friends and make sure you never do these things ever-fucking-again. Am. I. Clear?" I stare at the cocky one, keeping my tone controlled and cold.

His eyes break from mine first, and looks everywhere but at me.

"Yeah, that's what I thought. Fucking pussy," I growl.

No one says anything, and none of them look me in the eye. I snort at them, shake my head, and walk to the door. This time, I open it and keep going. My headache is pounding, and I need to sleep. For Destiny's sake, I hope they leave her alone.

CHAPTER 35

KAT

I'm sitting in my bedroom on my pink chaise lounge in my lingerie while the photographer takes discreet photos of me. Just another day of me being me, except this time, it's different.

Today is the day I marry Dane Reynolds, the only man who has ever made me feel safe and completely loved.

Dave is in the room too, checking and double-checking every photo to make sure I look good. These are only for Dane and me, but Dave is a perfectionist.

"Dave, I think we have enough photos of me in my underwear. Can I get dressed now, please?" I plead.

He looks at the photographer. "Do you think we

have enough?"

A sigh escapes my lips, and Sergio, the photographer, says, "Dave, you've had me take photos of her in just about every room in this house in her underwear. Yes, I think we have enough." Then he looks down at me. "But don't get dressed yet. I need a couple of shots of Jasmin and Rosie, then I'll send Jasmin in here to help you dress, and we'll shoot it as she does. Okay?"

Groaning, I stand, walk over to my robe and shove my arms through the holes. "Fine! But my face is about to crack from all the smiles."

Sergio flashes a grin. "Yes, it's hard to walk and smile while I click away in every known position to man." He jumps onto the chaise lounge, points the camera at me, and clicks away.

"You have a point, now get out!" I playfully yell at him as I point to the door.

Dave and I watch him leave, and I sit down on my side of the bed. After a moment, he joins me.

"You okay?" he asks.

"I'm fine, and I know this day is going to go quickly, but I want to get there. I want to see Dane, and I want the piece of paper that says he's mine."

Dave chuckles. "Princess, I don't think that's what it says. Besides, you'd have to be blind not to see how devoted the man is to you."

"He is, isn't he?" I say dreamily.

Dave nods, and I know in my heart, Dane would

never hurt me. I clasp Dave's hand and continue, "I'm glad you invited Luther, he's lovely."

Dave pats my hand. "Yes, he is. I'm surprised he came. I thought he'd say no, considering he lives in Hawaii."

"Hell, no! Have you seen how good you look in that suit! The navy blue brings out the color in your eyes. You look good, honey." I beam up at him.

A slight blush creeps up his neck. He stands and walks toward the mirror, admiring himself. "I look good, don't I?" Modesty has never been Dave's strong suit.

I giggle. "Yes! Let's go find something to eat that won't wreck this makeup. I'm hungry."

He grabs my hand again, and we make our way toward the kitchen. Dave hired caterers to look after us this morning and even organized them for Dane at the clubhouse.

"Ms. Saunders, what can we get you?" asks a woman dressed in black.

"Do we have any fruit? And maybe some bubbles?"

"Of course." She snaps her fingers, and there's a flurry of people running to appease her.

A server places a glass in my hand as another fills it up, and within moments, a selection of fruit is placed on the kitchen table. There are heaps to choose from—strawberries, mangoes, kiwi, and all the berries in the family. Just as I'm about to pick up a strawberry, I hear a sound from outside. I look out on the deck, and Rosie and Jas are out there having their photos taken. Rosie is wearing a red, off-the-shoulder, mid-length dress with a wide black ribbon tied at the waist. Her shoes complement the dress—they also have black ribbon which laces across her feet and ties at the back of her heel. She's positively glowing and I'm so happy she's coming as Truth's date. Jas is wearing a halter-neck navy dress which goes to the floor with a slit up to her thigh. She looks gorgeous. Both women are dressed and ready for my wedding.

Walking to the sliding door, I pull it open, then walk out. "How come they are dressed and not in their underwear?"

Rosie goes bright red while Jasmine bursts out laughing. Sergio cocks an eyebrow at me. "The lingerie photos are only for you and Dane, or do you think he'd prefer some with these lovely ladies?"

"No, he wouldn't," I say sheepishly.

Sergio shakes his head at me and continues to click away. Jasmin walks to me, takes my bubbles out of my hand, and drinks it in one go. I hadn't even had a sip yet. Just as I'm about to open my mouth to complain, a server comes running out with a tray of champagne flutes filled with bubbles, and we all take one.

"Now, that's what I call service." Jasmin looks the server in the eye. "You want to move into my house and do this for me all the time?"

"No, he fucking doesn't," says Judge as he walks out through the sliding doors.

There's an edge to his voice I haven't heard before, and although he's smiling, you know he means business. Jasmin walks toward him and throws her arms around his neck.

Judge is in jeans and has a white shirt on with a blue sports coat, and I have no doubt Jasmin asked him to wear it.

"Nice jacket! You look sharp," I gush at him.

He unlocks Jasmin's arms from around his neck, steps back, and turns with his arms wide. "Yeah, sugar, I scrub up well."

"Hmm… yes you do," agrees Dave with a wink.

For a moment, Judge looks like he doesn't know how to handle Dave's compliment.

"Hands off, manager man, this one's mine!" cries Jasmin, wrapping her arms around Judge's waist.

Sergio is still clicking away at Rosie, who's smiling at me.

"Rosie, I don't think I've ever seen you look more beautiful," I say.

She smiles shyly. "Truth picked it for me. I feel like a princess."

I place an arm around her shoulders. "He has good taste. About time he got it right in the female department, too."

Her face goes a deeper shade of red. "Thank you

so much for letting me stay here, Kat. I'm sorry if I've been an inconvenience."

Laughter escapes me, and I let her go. "Honey, you have been nothing but a help to me! You've also kept Truth in line. Any woman who can do that is a friend of mine."

"Amen to that!" teases Jasmin, who's still wrapped around Judge.

Another server comes out onto the deck with a platter of fruit, and we all congregate around it. I pick up a toothpick and stab a small strawberry. Sergio continues to take photos as we chat and eat.

"Sugar, shouldn't you be getting ready?" asks Judge.

"According to our world-famous photographer, Jasmin needs to help me, so he can take *more* photos." I roll my eyes.

"Come on then, Kat, let's get the dress on you." Jasmin walks away from Judge, grabs my hand, and leads me back to my bedroom.

Inside our walk-in closet hangs my ivory dress. The crystal beads catch in the light as I carefully take it off the coat hanger and carry it to the bed. It has a high lace neck going down into small, capped sleeves. The bodice hugs my body and fans out at the knees, emphasizing my hourglass figure. I had it made as I wanted something flattering for my body shape, but as I'm self-conscious about it, it needed to cover the scar on my neck. The dress is everything I wanted and more.

"Oh, Kat, it's beautiful," whispers Jasmin.

I nod and smile. "They did a good job, didn't they?"

Sergio bursts into the bedroom. "Good! You haven't started! That Rosie is a photographer's dream. The photos of her and Truth together... well, I can't explain it. Here, look at them. They are perfect." He passes us his camera, and we look at the photos of them together.

"Oh boy, Truth is hooked! Look at his face in this one!" Jasmin says.

In the photo, Rosie is staring straight ahead, but Truth is staring at her. Even from his profile, there's nothing but pure adoration on his face.

"Yes! It's like *Beauty and the Beast*." Both of us look at Sergio questioningly. "Well, he's covered in tattoos and looks dark, but she's all innocence and light. They really make a stunning couple."

"I can see that," agrees Jasmin.

"He seems smitten," I say.

"She's been staying out here for a few days in his room, and he hasn't..." Jasmin goes quiet.

"He hasn't?" I ask incredulously.

"No, apparently he wants to get to know her. You ever heard of Truth doing that before?"

"*Never*, Jas."

"Ladies, could I have my camera back, please? It's obvious he really likes her. Perhaps she's not simply a conquest to him, but something a bit deeper?"

"Truth doesn't do deeper," I say as I hand the camera back.

"Have you noticed he doesn't give her pet names?" I look quizzically at Jasmin. "You know, curious Kat, my rebellious rocker," she says seductively.

"You're right, he doesn't. She's only Rosie. So, he must be serious?"

"Ladies, as fascinating as this conversation is, could we have it *while* you're putting the dress on?" urges Sergio.

Jasmin shrugs at him. "Sergio, this is important stuff here. Truth doesn't *do* what Truth is *doing*."

"Kat hit the nail on the head when she said he's smitten," Sergio continues. "Now, Jasmine, pick up the dress and smile at Kat." He looks to me, "Kat, take off the robe and smile."

"Sounds like a porno, Sergio." I laugh at him.

"We don't have time for that. Maybe next time?" he suggests.

"I'm not doing this again. This is a one-time gig for me. There's only one Dane Reynolds in the world, and soon, he will be mine."

Jasmin picks up the dress. "Shall we, then?"

With her help, I step into my gown as she begins the arduous task of doing up all the buttons which run down the back of it. Sergio is clicking away, but after Jasmin does up the tenth button at the back, she stops, kneels behind me, and begins doing them up from the bottom.

"How many freaking buttons *are* on this thing?" whines Jasmin.

"Stop complaining and keep going, we're almost there." I can feel Sergio smiling.

When they are finally finished, I turn around.

"Kat, you look beautiful. I'm sure there's never been a more beautiful bride," whispers Jasmin.

Sergio stops and looks at me. "Yeah, and it hides the scar at your neck perfectly." Both of us pin him with a death stare, and he takes a step back, confused by our hostility. "What? It does."

I shake my head at him, and Jasmin picks up a small pillow off my bed and throws it at him.

"You're a regular Mr. Sensitive, aren't you?"

"I meant it as a compliment!" cries Sergio.

"It's okay, Jasmin. It's one of the reasons I had the dress made, so Sergio is technically right."

Dave walks into the room. "Princess, you look beautiful!" Tears well in his eyes.

"Oh no, no, no! You cry, then she cries, then the makeup is ruined!" yells Jasmin, pushing him out of the room.

I look at Sergio, who's grinning. "Come on, Kat, time to make you an old married lady."

CHAPTER 36

DANE

I'm standing at the bar of the clubhouse while a photographer takes what must be my millionth photo. I've almost had enough. Jonas is at the other end of the bar, dressed in a similar black suit with a white shirt. I have a red tie on, and he has a navy blue one to match Jasmin, the bridesmaid.

The red is for Kat's bouquet. I know she's wearing ivory, but that's all she'd tell me. MC weddings are normally a little less formal, but for my woman, I'd do anything. She wanted a big day, so she's going to get a big day.

Jonas slides a beer down to me, and I catch it. I smile at the photographer and take a swig.

"That's perfect, Mr. Reynolds! Could we do it again?" shrieks the photographer.

"No."

"Come on, Dane, we need to get you to the chapel on time." Jonas is my best man. He's my oldest friend and knows more about me than anyone. "You nervous?"

I shake my head. "No, brother. Just want the circus to be over."

"She's a hell of a woman, but I'm not sure I'd go through all of this for anyone," he smirks.

"Not even if Addy asked you to?"

He pauses and shakes his head. "We aren't there yet, brother. I'll cross that bridge when I get to it."

I laugh at him. "We'll see."

"Are you ready to leave?" I nod. "Okay, let's get this show on the road."

We walk out of the clubhouse and down to our bikes. I climb on and let out a large whistle, and the gates to the compound slowly open.

I look at Jonas. "Are you ready to face all those people?"

He looks up and shrugs. "So long as they get out of the way, and we get to the church on time, I'm ready for anything."

The photographer is still with us and keeps clicking away. I raise an eyebrow at him. "How are you getting to the church?"

"I'll be in my car taking photos as you ride in, and my assistant will drive me." He smiles.

I was hoping I'd lose him here, but I can see that's

not going to happen. I look at Jonas, who says, "Come on, Dane. You know Kat will want photos of you on your bike. Let it happen, go with the flow." One day I'm going to wipe that grin off his face.

Grunting at him, I start my bike, and Jonas follows suit. I'm not waiting for the photographer, so I head for the gate. Getting through the throng of press and onlookers isn't as easy as I thought it would be. We get held up for a good ten minutes trying to get through. In the end, my MC makes a hole, and we speed off with the photographer hot on our heels.

When we reach the church, there are more people here than at the compound. I get off my bike and throw my keys at a prospect as Jonas does the same to another. They're returning our bikes to the compound now, so we won't have to worry about them later.

Jonas slaps me on the back. "You ready?"

"You got the ring?"

He feels his breast pocket. "Sure do."

"Then, yes, my best man, I'm ready."

Shoulder to shoulder, we walk up the stairs and into the church. The Father comes up to me and shakes my hand. "Perfect day for a wedding, Dane. Now, if you'll come this way?" He grabs me by the elbow and motions for me to walk up the aisle.

The church is filled with many town folk and people I don't recognize that Kat must've invited.

She said there would be a lot of people from the music industry here. The only family I have here is my sister, Emily, and her family. She's sitting in the front row, on my side, looking beautiful in a pale pink dress. Salvatore has a possessive arm around her, with Vincent sitting on his lap.

Now I'm nervous, my blood is pumping a little faster, and I feel sweat beading on my upper lip. The Father positions me near the altar and guides Jonas to the right spot, too.

"Now, Dane, I want you to face forward until you hear the music start, then when it does, you can turn around and see the vision which will be your bride." He's grinning and seems perfectly at ease, but I suppose he's done this hundreds of times.

I can't get myself to speak, so I nod once and look straight ahead at the intricate woodwork of the church. Jonas chuckles beside me. I glare at him out of the corner of my eye, but he's staring straight ahead, too.

I couldn't imagine standing up here without him. He's a good friend—my best friend. He's protected me from all manner of threats and celebrated all of my accomplishments. For me, there was no higher honor I could bestow on him when I asked him to be my best man. To stand in front of God and the MC as I claim Katarina Saunders as my wife.

CHAPTER 37

DAVE

Kat looks regal sitting in the back of the limousine while Jasmin, for once, is quiet. It's only the three of us.

"You know I love you two, and it's my honor, Kat, to give you away today. I know your thoughts are probably with your mother, but she'd be so proud of you. I'll admit, I had my reservations about Dane, but over the last couple of years, I have never seen anyone make you so happy." I glance at Jasmin, and she has tears in her eyes. "Jasmin, honey, don't ruin *your* makeup. Dab those eyes now."

She sniffles, opens her bag, and pulls out tissues. She hands one to Kat, too. I grin at Kat, who has sadness in her eyes.

"I miss her, Dave. I wish she were here to see

this. I think she'd have gotten a kick out of me getting married in this little town." She dabs her eyes and forces a smile on her face.

"No tears today unless they are joyful ones!" I admonish her.

Her forced smile turns into a genuine smile. "Yes, Dave."

The limousine slows, looking out the tinted windows, there are people clamoring around the car. I hear all the doors lock, and the driver rolls down the glass between him and us.

"I'm sorry, Mr. Lawrence, I don't want to risk running anyone over so I'm taking it easy."

"That's fine. We certainly don't need any casualties today! Besides, the bride should be late for her own wedding. It's tradition." The driver rolls the screen back up, and we're alone again.

Jasmin has her compact out and is checking her face. "Kat, I love your veil. It goes perfectly with your dress."

Kat fingers the material. "It was my mother's. I had them sew some beads into it to match the dress. It works, doesn't it?"

"Yes, princess, with the tiara and your hair pulled off your face, you look like an angel."

"Dave, I think I prefer I look like a princess," Kat says with a grin.

"Yes, of course. Well, you look like a princess!" I say flamboyantly.

She giggles. "It's easy to remove the tiara and veil after the ceremony, but Jas, I'll need your help to make sure I don't mess my hair up too much."

"Baby, what else are bridesmaids for? Of course, I'll help. Now, do we need to have the sex talk?" teases Jasmin.

I nearly choke, and Kat bursts out laughing. I shake my head at Jasmin, who smiles and shrugs at me.

The limousine comes to a halt, and the driver again rolls down the screen. "We're at the church. Are you ready?"

I look at Kat, who takes a deep breath and nods. "I think we are."

The locks disengage and someone immediately opens the door.

"It's showtime, princess, and you're up!"

I climb out and stand on the sidewalk. The MC has a guard of honor down both sides of the walk up into the church, which thankfully keeps the fans away. I extend my hand to help Jasmin out of the limousine. Kat passes out her bouquet, which I hand to Jasmin. Then, my princess emerges. She grasps my hand with such force, I wince. Clearly, she's nervous. Jasmin hands her bouquet back to her and begins the walk into the church. I link my arm through Kat's, and we follow.

As we get to the top of the stairs, Kat stops and lets go of me. She turns and waves at the crowd. The cheers get louder, and the MC claps. That's my girl, always knows the right thing to do in front of an audience.

I place my hand on her waist, and she looks up at me. "Turn around, Dave, let's show off your gorgeous suit!"

I grin at her and do as I'm told. "Your man will hear the commotion, honey, and he'll be wondering what you're doing. You don't want Dane barreling down the aisle looking to protect you."

"Okay, let's do this."

She turns back around, and we step through the doors. Jasmin smiles at us, then we hear the bridal march, and another set of doors open. Inside are all of Kat's and Dane's family and friends, and all eyes are on the bride.

Jasmin begins the slow walk down the aisle, and I watch as Dane slowly turns around to see his bride. A look of love washes over his features, nearly brings me to tears. I glance down at my girl, and she's staring at Dane, smiling.

The walk up the aisle is too short, and in no time, the Father is asking me, "Who gives this woman to be married to this man?"

I feel my throat constrict and am amazed I can say, "I do." A tear runs down my face as I place Kat's hand in Dane's. I look him in the eyes and am surprised to see his eyes are shining, too. I smile at him and step away. Luther, my date, is in the front row and grabs my hand, helping me into my seat.

The Father begins with, "Welcome, family and friends. We are gathered here today to join this man and this woman in holy matrimony. Today is a day for celebration as two hearts become one." He pauses and nods to Dane, who looks to Jonas for the ring. "Okay, folks, here we go, the couple has memorized their vows, and I'm only up here to make sure it all runs smoothly."

A ripple of laughter goes through the crowd, and the priest winks at Dane.

Dane grasps Kat's hand, holding the wedding band on her finger, and says, "I, Dane Reynolds, take you, Katarina Saunders, to be my wife, my partner in life, and my one true love. I will cherish our union and love you more each day than I did the day before. I will trust you and respect you, laugh with you and cry with you, loving you faithfully through good times and bad, regardless of the obstacles we may face together. I give you my hand, my heart, and my love from this day forward for as long as we both shall live."

I have tears coursing down my face, and Luther hands me a handkerchief with a chuckle. I dab my eyes and only have eyes for the happy couple.

Kat, ever the performer, raises her voice so everyone in the church can hear. "I, Katarina Saunders, take you, Dane Reynolds, to be my husband, my partner in life, and my one and only *true* love. I will cherish our union and love you more each day than I did the day before. I will trust you and respect you, laugh with you and cry with you, loving you faithfully through good times and bad, regardless of the obstacles we may face, but baby, we'll face it all together." Laughter filters around the church. "I give you my hand, my heart and my love from this day forward for as long as we both shall live and then I'll love until the sun shines no more."

The Father grins at her then looks to Dane. "You may now kiss the bride..."

Dane lifts the veil on my princess, her smile so huge she radiates happiness.

For a big man, I watch as he lightly clasps her face, but the kiss is anything but gentle. Jonas howls, and the rest of the MC and some guests clap and cheer. When he finally breaks away from Kat, they only have eyes for each other, sharing a secret smile.

The Father places a hand on both of them and says, "I now present Mr. and Mrs. Dane Reynolds!"

The cheers get louder, and I'm on my feet, clapping. The happy couple turns and begins walking out of the church. Dane stops at his sister, Emily, who's opposite me, and leans down, whispering something to her. Kat comes up to me and kisses my cheek.

"Best show *ever*, princess!"

Kat looks so happy. "Thank you, Dave. Thank you for all your help."

Dane grabs her hand, and he leads my princess out of the church.

CHAPTER 38

DANE

When Kat entered the church and the music played, I turned around to look at her, and all the air got sucked out of my lungs. I don't think I started breathing again until Dave put her small hand in mine.

Throughout the ceremony, I studied her face, and at the end when the Father presented us to the church, I felt relief. This amazing woman is mine. I think in some small corner of my mind, I thought she might not come, or leave and never return. The reception is in the town hall, which has tables spread throughout it with flowers on each one and the chairs all have large bows on the backs of them. Kat is doing the rounds of our guests, smiling, shaking hands, but every so often her eyes seek me out and she smiles at me, warming my heart, making me love her more. I'm standing with a group of my brothers, who are giving me shit, and for once, I'm taking it. Right now, I don't care about a damn thing.

As I look around the room, I see Adelynn and Jonas on the dance floor, swaying to the music. Emily is sitting on Salvatore's knee, watching Vincent run around as they whisper to each other. Truth has Rosie in an embrace as he talks to someone in the music industry. He hasn't let her take more than three steps away from him all evening. Dave is in deep conversation with Luther, who isn't anything like Dave at all. He's not flamboyant, and if you didn't know he was gay, you'd think he was straight.

"Hey, Prez, your woman looks good," says Judge as he motions to Kat.

"Yes, she does." I point at Jasmin. "Jas looks good, too. You two seem more... together than normal?" I ask with a smirk.

"Yeah, she's finally figured out I'm fantastic." He wiggles his eyebrows up and down at me, and laughter rumbles up and out of my chest.

He slaps me on the back and walks in Jasmin's direction. I watch as he hugs her from behind, and she giggles, then introduces him to whomever she's talking to. It's probably another music person.

The entire room looks like they're having fun. I

catch Kat's eye and motion for her to meet me on the other side of the room. She's talking to someone, but gives me a slight nod. I walk toward the other side of the room, and she meets me halfway. I grab her hand, and we step out into a nearly vacant hallway.

"Darlin', who the fuck are all these people?"

"Musicians, industry people. They all want to meet you, but you've been hanging out with the brothers. You need to mingle, honey. Do it for me?" She flutters her eyes and pouts at me.

"How can a man say fucking no to that? All right, take me to your people."

She giggles. "They are *our* people now."

As we walk across the floor toward a group of people smiling expectantly at us, I hear someone popping the cork off a bottle of champagne as someone screams.

"Everyone, this is my husband, Dane Reynolds."

I shake some hands and look at Kat. "I like the sound of that," I murmur to Kat, who smiles at me.

Another bottle of champagne is popped, and Kat jumps. I laugh at her, but her face has gone slack.

"Darlin'?"

She's holding her side, and when she pulls her hand away, it's covered in crimson.

"Dane?" Her face is a mask of confusion.

I take two steps toward her and grab her as she falls. I can hear more popping noises, and I realize it's gunfire. People are running in every direction. I cover her body with my own. I look up, and I can't get a bearing on where the bullets are coming from.

My eyes lock with Adelynn's, her hands are covered in blood, and she's screaming for someone to help her. Jonas' body is crumpled on the floor at her feet. A man lies lifeless only a foot from me. More gunshots sound out, but I can't see which direction they are coming from.

Screams pierce the air, and it feels like everything is going in slow motion. I smell blood, gunfire, and fear in the air. I look down at my Kat, and she's gasping. I pick her up and race, without fear for myself, to the other side of the room and back into the hallway. No one is there now.

"D... Dane, what's happened?" whispers Kat.

I brush her hair off her face. "I'm not sure yet. Kat, I need to lay you down and put pressure on your wound, okay?"

"I've been hit?" Her eyes flutter, and then they close.

I press my fingers to her throat and check her pulse, then lay her out on the floor, pull off my jacket, and place it under her head. Then I place my hands over her wound as blood seeps up between my fingers. Dirt finds me, he has his gun out, and his eyes are wild.

He looks at Kat and sees the blood on my shirt. "Are you hit?" he demands.

I shake my head, unable to speak as more blood coats my fingers.

He walks back into the main room. I hear a loud crash, and then he's back in front of me. "Whoever they are, they're either dead or gone. Let's get her up onto a table."

He tries to touch Kat, and I growl at him. No one will touch her. I pick her back up, and a groan parts her lips. We walk back into the main room, and I place my wife on a table. One of her shoes has fallen off, and I stupidly wonder where it is.

Judge stalks up to the table and places his fingers on Kat's throat. Without realizing it, I growl at him. "Be calm, brother, I was only checking on her."

"Casualties?" I demand.

"I haven't done a full assessment yet. I was trying to find you and Kat. Jonas and Truth are hit, and a wedding guest I don't know is dead. That's all I know. It all happened so fast."

Dirt hands me a cloth, and I push it against Kat's wound. I watch it turn from white to red instantly, and it feels like the life force is draining out of her. I hear sirens, and I look to Dirt.

"It's going to be all right, brother, she's going to be all right. I'll bring them to you." He hands his gun to Judge and runs toward the front of the building. I can hear women crying and groans all around me. As I stare down at Kat, her face has gone pale, and I fear I'm going to lose her.

Dirt comes running back into the room with two paramedics. I'm pushed away from her as they begin their life-saving efforts.

"How did they get here so fast?" I ask Dirt.

"Brother, people have been queuing up all day to get a glimpse of Kat. Some fainted earlier in the day, and it was decided to keep one bus here in town, just in case."

They load her onto a gurney and strap her in. I look at Dirt, but he's the first one to speak, "Go, brother, we'll handle this and give you an update soon." Dirt's face is full of concern. Without a second glance, I follow the paramedics to the ambulance.

CHAPTER 39

SHERIFF CARLOS MORALES

I was in the marquee at the front of the town hall when the first gunshot sounded. I yelled for everybody to get down as bullets flew around the room. The man who was sitting across from me got hit in the head, and I'm covered in his blood, brain matter, and bone. We're lucky more people weren't hit.

I'm looking for my men when a security guard runs up to me. "Sheriff, Kat Saunders got hit!"

"Is she all right?"

"Don't know, an ambulance took her away two minutes ago. There are more people wounded and more ambulances coming. What do you need me to do?" he asks.

"Are the assailants all accounted for?"

"We think so."

"Fuck! *We think so?*" I berate him.

A state trooper comes into the marquee and walks straight up to me. "Sheriff, all combatants are dead or down, and we have the area under control."

"How the fuck did this happen? Do we know who it was?" I have my hands on my hips, and I'm angry. I know it's not this trooper's fault, but he's the one I'm taking my frustrations out on.

"Sheriff, from what little info I know, it appears as if they killed one of your deputies who got in the way."

I feel the anger rise in me. "They killed one of *my* deputies? Who?"

"I believe it was Deputy Billy Barrett, sir."

Jesus, Billy was young, hadn't made his mark in the world yet. I look down at my shoes, then back up at the trooper. "Who's in charge?"

"Sheriff, it's your town. We're only here as a courtesy to you. My boss asked me to come find you so you could, and I quote, 'run this fiasco.'"

Great, they'll be looking for a scapegoat, someone to blame, and I guess I'm it. "Take me to him."

As I follow the trooper through the marquee, I see more bodies. There's a woman in a green dress with her head back and eyes open, but they hold no life. A man is sprawled on the ground with a pool of blood around him.

Everywhere I look, there's carnage.

When I reach the sidewalk, I see Addy covered in blood, tears streaming down her face. I pull off my jacket and place it around her shoulders.

"Are you hurt?"

She shakes her head. "Jonas was shot, they are working on him," she chokes out and points to where he is.

"Wait here. Trooper, wait with her," I order.

I move to where Jonas is, and he has a bullet wound to his shoulder and a nasty cut to the side of his head. "What's his status?"

When the man treating him looks up, I see it's our town doctor. "Bullet wound to his upper torso, but no exit wound, possible internal bleeding. Laceration to the head, possibly from a bullet, or he hit it on the way down on God knows what. We need to get him to a hospital. Now," commands Doc Jordan.

"What if we put him in the back of a cruiser?" I ask.

"We could meet the ambulance halfway. Let's get him into a car."

I run back to the trooper. "We need a police cruiser. You're going to take Doc Jordan and Jonas to the hospital. Hopefully, you'll meet an ambulance en-route, and they can take him the rest of the way."

He nods and runs off to get a car. I grab Addy by the shoulders. "Doc Jordan is going to need your help, okay, love?" She looks shaken but dips her head in the affirmative. "Good woman, now go, and I want you to call me if you need *anything*."

She rushes to Jonas' side, and I make my way toward the throng of law enforcement.

"What the fuck happened?" I bellow.

"The Minions of Death. We killed six of them and apprehended another two."

"A fucking MC war? Are you fucking kidding me?" I ask, not really expecting an answer. "Have we secured the perimeter?"

"Yes, sir!" yells a young trooper from the back.

"Let's make our way through the building, making sure we haven't missed a shooter or an injured person. You'll go in pairs. Now move!"

I grab one of my deputies as he walks by me. "Yes, Sheriff?"

"I need you to take photos of everything. Confiscate one of the cameras off one of the press if you have to. Hell, take a news cameraman around and document everything. This goes by the book, understand?"

"Yes, Sheriff." He's young, and he's rattled, but he does as he is told.

The next day, Tourmaline is flooded with more media than we know what to do with. It feels like the entire world is focusing on us. I've been up for over twenty-four hours trying to piece together what happened.

The Savage Angels had a run-in early last week with the Minions of Death, and it spilled over into my town. I'm surprised this MC had enough balls to go after the Savage Angels. They're a small club compared to them. War will surely follow, and I don't want any more bloodshed in my town.

A group of the town's people cornered one gunman before he could reload and beat him to death. Perhaps Reynolds was right, maybe we should call it Savage Town.

I'm sitting at my desk with my head in my hands when my phone rings. "Sheriff Morales."

"Carlos? It's Addy." She sounds tired and broken.

"Are you all right?"

"I'm exhausted and can't sleep. They took Jonas back in for more surgery, but they tell me he's now stabilized, and it looks good." I hear her sniffle. "Kat's another story. They're saying she won't make it. Apparently, she coded twice in the ambulance, but they brought her back. It's not looking good for her," her voice cracks, and she goes silent. I hear her sobbing on the other end of the line.

"Addy, deep breaths. I'm glad Jonas is going to be fine, honey. You concentrate on him. Kat Saunders,

I mean Kat Reynolds is tough, don't count her out just yet."

"Do we know why this happened?" she chokes out.

"Not really, it's too soon. Addy, I have to go. Will you be all right? Do you need me to do anything?"

"No, Carlos, I'm fine. I only needed to hear a friendly voice."

"Bye, Addy." I hang up.

I'm lost in my own thoughts as to what could've been between Addy and me when there's a tap at my door.

Standing in the doorway is the mayor of Tourmaline, Justice Leaverton. He, too, is still in a tuxedo and looks like he hasn't slept.

"Do we know how many are dead, Sheriff? We need to give a statement to the press."

"I don't give a flying fuck about the press. Let them wait!" I snarl at him.

"Carlos, you know we have to. Might as well get it done now. Go have a shower and change into your uniform. I told them you would give them a debriefing in an hour."

"And if I say no?" I say with no small amount of hostility.

"Carlos, the whole-fucking-world is staring at us right now. I've heard fifty people were killed. If we let that kind of ridiculous reporting go on, it's bad for the town."

I know he's right. We need to get in front of this, but it irks me this happened at all.

"I have a uniform in my closet, and I can shower here. Are you going to stand with me while I give my statement, Mr. Mayor?"

He lets out a sigh. "I thought I'd say something before you give your briefing, if it's all right?"

I nod, open my closet, and get out a uniform. "Of course, see you in twenty."

He moves out of my way, and I head to the shower rooms.

I take my time in the shower and shave as well. By the time I come back out to my office, it's been thirty minutes, and I feel semi-human. Justice has combed his hair, but his usual cheerful disposition has been replaced with a pensive one.

"Mr. Mayor, if you'd lead the way?" I ask.

He walks ahead of me through the bullpen, and out the front doors to the waiting press. A hush goes over the crowd as Justice walks up to the podium. The press cameras flash, and the red light indicates it's being broadcast to live televisions everywhere.

"To my fellow citizens of Tourmaline and everyone else who has been affected by this tragedy. This unfortunate incident isn't a reflection on our great town." He pauses, and it looks as though he's struggling to find the words. "But rather a re-enforcement that gang violence will not be tolerated in any form, those who perpetrated this heinous, cowardly act will pay for what they have done along with those who ordered them to do it!"

The press fires out questions, but he moves to the side of the podium and motions for me to take center stage.

I stand there and wait for the press to quiet down. I stare out over them and can see many of the town's folk at the back of them.

I sigh. "This is the worst incident this town has ever known. We have three locals dead, including my own, Deputy Billy Barrett. We haven't contacted the families of the other two, so I'm not releasing their names at this time. Five guests at the wedding and six armed assailants..." I pause as questions are thrown at me. I hold up my hands, and they quiet down again. "Eight people were taken to the hospital, and many more were treated at the scene for minor injuries. Katarina Saunders was shot and is in critical condition. I ask that you respect her and her family and..." again, I pause this time searching for the right words, but they fail me, "... keep the hell away from them. They have enough to worry about right now and don't need you assholes bothering them."

The crowd goes silent, then I hear clapping from someone at the back of the crowd. I think it's Howie from the café, but I can't be sure. Pretty soon, everyone in the back is clapping, and as the press calls out questions, I turn on my heel and stalk back into my station.

CHAPTER 40

DANE

It's been three days since the shootings. Kat is still in critical condition, the doctors don't think she has much hope of surviving, and I feel like my world is pulling apart at the seams. Salvatore is sitting next to me. Emily went into labor after the shooting stopped and delivered a healthy baby girl. He hasn't left Emily's side, but he told me she ordered him to come and sit with me.

We're sitting outside the intensive care unit. I haven't been able to move or sleep. I haven't eaten anything. All I've done is pray silently to myself.

"How does it feel to be an uncle again?" asks Sal.

I turn my head slightly in his direction. "Hadn't given it any thought."

"Would you like to know your niece's name?"

I shrug.

"We decided on this before the... accident. We're going to call her Dana Katarina Agostino."

"It wasn't an accident. It was a fucking hit, and they were looking for me. They say she probably won't survive, Sal." My words are raw, and emotion gets the best of me. Standing, I punch a wall, splintering the plaster.

Sal rests his hand on my shoulder. "I couldn't imagine a life without Emily or Vincent. But what you're doing right now would piss Kat off. She's not dead yet, you need to remember that."

I drop my fist and nod, then resume my position on the chair. My knuckles are bleeding. A nurse walks past, looks at the hole in the wall, then at me. She doesn't stop but is back a few moments later with iodine and swabs.

"Give me your hand," she demands.

I look up at her with empty eyes and hold out my hand. I don't even flinch when she cleans my wounds. The pain is nothing compared to not having Kat in my life. She opens her mouth to say something, then closes it and goes back to her station.

For a while, we sit in silence.

"How is Jonas, do you know?"

"He's going to make it."

I don't see the need to make small talk, and thankfully Sal doesn't push.

A doctor comes running past us and into Kat's room. I stand and walk to her doorway. She's convulsing on the bed, and the doctor is yelling out instructions and trying to hold her down. Eventually, it stops, and the alarms on all the machines she's hooked up to go back to their normal rhythms.

The doctor is reading her chart and writing things on it. I walk into the room, glaring at him. His eyes flick to me and then to the nurses still in the room.

"Will she live?"

"She's lost a lot of blood. The convulsion was due to a spike in temperature. Her body is fighting off an infection. We've repaired her body as best we can, the rest is up to her."

Reaching down, I pick up her hand. "Darlin', I need you to wake up. I can't take much more of this." I bring her hand to my lips. "Do you hear me, Kat? Please wake up. I need you to wake up."

The doctor clears his throat, and I glance at him. "Keep talking to her. Some say they can't hear you, but I've had patients wake up and tell me about conversations they've had with loved ones. Your voice might be what brings her back." He offers a half-smile and leaves.

I drag a seat over to the bed and place her hand back in mine. "Kat, darlin', you've been asleep for three days. It's long enough. Wake the fuck up."

Anger washes over me, and I can't speak. I close my eyes, put the back of her hand to my forehead, and pray.

CHAPTER 41

DIRT

The entire town went to the funerals of the locals who died. It's been a week since the murders, and we needed to put our dead to rest. All the shops are closed, and we all paid our respects. I was worried we'd get blamed for the incident, but the town seems to be defending us to outsiders and anyone else who tries to discredit us.

As an MC, we, of course, helped with the cleanup of the Town Hall and park after the sheriff had finished with it. The sheriff blames us. He lost one of his own and isn't in a forgiving frame of mind. I've tried to start a conversation with him, but it's still too raw for him, and he wants no part of us. I don't blame him.

Many in our chapter wanted a war, but it turns

out, it was only eight of the Minions who decided to teach us a lesson for the beat-down Kade and his boys gave them. As much as we wanted blood for what happened, it would've been futile. They lost six men, and another two are in jail. Fourteen people died, and for what?

Nothing.

I know Kade feels responsible, but it's not his fault. He hasn't been to see Dane, and the longer he puts it off, the harder it will be for him.

I had a sit-down with the Minions of Death, who asked what they could do to make this right. It's a good question, but in all honesty, *nothing* can make this right. Fourteen people died because some asshole tried to take out the president of the Savage Angels MC. He tried and failed and is one of the dead.

I'm thinking about all of this as I walk back into the hospital. Dane refuses to leave Kat's side and isn't eating. He's even in the same clothes he had on when he got married. When I get into the elevator, a woman looks at my jacket and gets out. People who aren't from Tourmaline fear us now.

Walking the familiar corridors to Kat's room, I find Dane muttering to himself as I stand at the threshold.

"Hey, brother, time for you to shower and change."

His red-rimmed eyes look up at me, and he gives

a slight shake of his head. "No."

"If you don't, they are going to kick you out of here. That surly nurse who patched your hand said you can use the bathroom in one of the vacant rooms two floors down."

"Not leaving her."

"I'll stay with her, but you *are* going."

He snarls at me. "I'll hurt you, Dirt, if you try to make me leave."

I look up at the nurse and give a slight shake of my head. She walks away, only to come into the room a short time later.

She places a hand on Dane's shoulder. "When was the last time you slept, Mr. Reynolds?"

"I'll sleep when she wakes up."

She smiles at me and appears to be playing with something in her pocket. The nurse points at one of the monitors and says, "Is it always like that?"

Both of us turn to look, and she stabs Dane in the arm with a needle, then takes two steps back. "I'm sorry, Mr. Reynolds, I really am. But you aren't doing yourself any favors by not sleeping or eating."

Dane stands, twirls around to face her, his knees buckle, and he face-plants it to the floor. He's out cold.

The nurse looks up at me. "I'm sorry, but he really needs to sleep. He'll thank me for it in the long run."

"Not fucking likely, love. He's going to be pissed."

"Really?" She looks down at his massive frame. "Well, I'm owed a heap of holidays. Might be time to get out of town for a while?"

I nod at her and say, "Sounds good, but what are we going to do with him?"

She walks out into the hallway and motions for an orderly. "Go get a wheelchair, and let's get this poor, exhausted man into it."

We get him into a wheelchair when Rebel walks into the room. "What the fuck? Is he all right?"

The nurse nervously says, "He collapsed from exhaustion. I'm taking him to a room to sleep it off."

"Reb, go with her and keep an eye on Dane. No one gets near him. I'm going to stay here with Kat until he wakes up. He wouldn't want her left alone," I explain.

Reb gives me one last look then they all leave, and I look down at Kat's still form. Reaching out, I touch her hand, and I'm surprised at how cold it feels. I pull the blankets up and tuck them around her, then I sit in Dane's seat and clasp her hand between mine.

"You feel cold, love. We need you to wake up. Did Dane tell you, you're an aunty again? They called her Dana Katarina, poor kid." I chuckle. "If life wasn't hard enough, they had to name her after the pair of you? That's some big shoes to fill." Her hand twitches, and I look at her face, but nothing's there. "Jonas is fine. He's sitting up, wanting to know when he can leave. Addy is doing everything for him. It's funny to see him being bossed around. Remember when Dane got hurt? Well, I think she's worse than you were." I chuckle, remembering how Kat wouldn't let Dane do anything.

My thoughts drift, and I think about Kat's ma and our first encounter with her. She made me look bad in front of the whole MC, and eventually, we became friends. Her death was a shock to me, and even though we've since discovered she wasn't who we thought she was, she was a good friend. Then, I remember how Kat came to be in our lives, how the loss of not only her singing voice but her mother bought her right to us. Sometimes, the plan is bloody, messy, and painful, and we don't know what the Almighty is thinking, but He always has a plan for us.

I look at my watch, and I've been sitting here, lost in my thoughts, for over an hour. I let go of her and stand, stretching out my lower back muscles. As I turn around, I see Kade waiting outside. I motion for him to come in, but he walks to the door and stops.

"How long have you been out there?" I ask.

"A little while. I'm not sure how long. Where's Dane?"

"He's sleeping two floors down. Rebel is with him."

"Didn't think he'd leave her side," says Kade,

motioning to Kat.

"You could call it an intervention. I had a chat with one of the nurses, and she may have helped him fall asleep."

"He's not going to like it," replies Kade.

"No, brother, he won't. Could you sit with Kat while I go find a restroom? Dane won't want her left alone."

"Yes, brother, I can sit with her."

I nod at him. "Want me to bring you back a coffee?"

"Yeah, black, no sugar," he says, eyes glued to Kat.

I slap him on the back and leave the room.

CHAPTER 42

KADE

I sit in the chair next to Kat's bed and watch her chest rise and fall slowly with the machines. Her face is pale, and with her hair spread out over the pillow, she looks like an angel.

"It was my fault, Kat. I had an altercation with the Minions of Death, and they sought revenge. They were after Dane, but you were in the way."

I lean forward, placing my elbows on my knees, and link my hands together. I can't look at her, but I continue to ramble. "None of our MC were killed. The fucking press is everywhere. Dane hasn't left your side." I scrub a hand over my face and sit back, avoiding looking at her. "He's not going to enjoy being separated from you."

A nurse comes in and checks her vitals, and for a

time, I sit there and don't speak.

When she leaves, I say, "I wouldn't even be here now if it wasn't for Fith. If he had told Dane where the fucking loft was before he died, I'd be long gone. In a way, this all goes back to your mother. If she'd never met any of us, Fith would be alive, and you probably wouldn't even have crossed our path. It's weird the way lives get intertwined. Dane won't survive losing you. There's something broken in him, and if you don't come out of this, I don't think we'll get him back." I sigh and stand, still avoiding looking at her. "Katarina Reynolds, as you're now an official Old Lady, I'm telling you to wake the fuck up."

The heart rate monitor beeps and speed up for a moment, I look at Kat's face. There's nothing there, no flicker of emotion.

"That's not good enough, Kat. You can do better than fucking that." I stare at the machine, but there's no increase.

"I haven't tried swearing at her. Is it working?" Dave asks.

His face is haggard from lack of sleep.

I point at the machine. "It went crazy for a moment, and I thought..."

"You thought swearing at her might help?" He takes two steps into the room, grips the metal bar at the end of the bed, and yells, "Katarina, showtime! Get your ass up! Then it's booze, parties, and a well-fucking-deserved vacation for everyone!" Tears course down his face, and it's a mask of pain.

A nurse runs into the room and looks at us. "What's going on?"

"He thought swearing might help, but I thought yelling might be better, so I combined the two," explains Dave without looking at her. "Wake the fuck up, Kat, this has gone on long enough!" roars Dave, shaking the bed.

I shake my head at the nurse and escort her out of the room. "We'll keep it down," I tell her, but I have no idea how I'm supposed to make Dave do that.

Dave is openly crying at the end of the bed, and his knuckles are going white as they grip onto it.

"Dave, you need to calm down. They'll throw us out of here if we make too much fucking noise. Sit down, take the chair."

He nods and lets go of the bed. My gaze goes back to Kat, and her eyes are open, staring at me.

"Nurse!" I bellow, running out into the hall.

The same nurse comes running into the room. Dave is up and hovering over Kat. The nurse looks at Kat, presses a button near the bed, and yells with no small amount of authority. "Everybody out! Now!" Then she turns her attention back to Kat.

Both of us stumble backward out of the room as a doctor and another nurse run in. I look to my left and see Dirt walking toward us. He drops the coffees and runs the rest of the way. Dave drops to his knees as Dirt gets to us.

"Is she dead?" asks Dirt, staring at Dave.

"No, brother, she's awake. Dave yelled at her to wake up, and she did," I say.

Dirt hugs me. "Well, why the fuck didn't I think of that?"

We help Dave to his feet and wait impatiently for the doctor to come out. We watch as they remove the tube from her throat and run tests on her. She's nodding slowly but not talking. Eventually, the doctor comes out to us.

"She's awake. We have an oxygen mask on her, and she may not be able to speak for a little while, and if she does, it could be hoarse. She still needs bed rest. I don't want you all wearing her out. So, one at a time. Where's her husband?" he asks, looking at all of us.

"I'll go find him," says Dirt as he runs away.

"Dave, she'll want to see your face more than mine. Get in there."

Silent tears fall, as he goes to her. I watch as Kat struggles to lift a hand, and he clasps it quickly. Dave is openly sobbing, holding onto her, unable to speak.

The doctor is back in the room writing on her chart, and I stand in the doorway.

Her eyes keep darting from Dave to me, and

eventually, Dave says, "Kade, I think she wants to talk to you."

She nods slightly. He kisses her hand and walks out of the room. She tries to pull the mask off her face.

The doctor puts it back over her mouth. "You need to keep this on, Ms. Saunders."

"Her name is *Mrs.* Reynolds," I say with more force than necessary.

He raises his eyebrows but says nothing and goes back to her chart.

Kat again reaches for the mask and whispers, "Closer." I have my head tilted, and I get as close to her mouth as I dare, she says, "Lower Oconee Fire Trail... loft."

Fuck me, loft isn't a fucking loft, it's an acronym. This entire time I've been looking in the wrong fucking place.

I smile down at her. "Thank you."

"Darlin'?" A very groggy Dane stumbles through the doorway, and I back out. He lightly clasps her face in his hands as tears escape her eyes.

"Don't you *ever* fucking do that to me again, darlin', you hear me?" Kat nods at him, and he kisses her forehead.

I look at Dirt, Rebel, and Dave, who have huge smiles on their faces. Being in an MC isn't all about the brotherhood. It also includes our girlfriends, wives, children, and all the people we come in contact with.

"I'm going to go see Jonas and tell him the good news. Rebel, do you want to go downstairs and tell everyone waiting down there Kat's awake?"

"Yeah, man, I do." He punches Dirt and runs for the elevator.

I hold my hand out to Dave, who grasps it. "If I'd known swearing, yelling, and shaking her bed would have worked, I would've asked you to do it sooner."

He grins at me. "My boy, if *I'd* known about it, I would have done it sooner."

"What the fuck are you two on about?" asks Dirt.

"Dave here woke our girl up." I slap Dave on the shoulder and walk toward the elevator.

I hear Dave say, "It's true, it was all me."

As I enter the elevator to go to Jonas' room, I look at myself on the reflective surface and realize I'm grinning.

EPILOGUE

DANE

It's been three months since our wedding and three months since Kat's shooting. She's at home now, but keeping her in bed and inactive hasn't been easy. None of her family has left her side, and they've started writing songs for an upcoming album they've decided to release. Curtis has already done some work on it with a new sound for them.

When I walk into our bedroom, carrying coffee for the two of us, she's surrounded by our family. It's driving me a little crazy. It's like no one can move past the shooting, and we all need to hold on to each other for a little while longer. I wish they'd get out of our bedroom. Kat holds out a hand for her coffee and I pass it to her. The others are all sitting around the room, on the bed, on the floor, chatting to each other as though it's the most normal thing in the world to be in our bedroom. We don't take our eyes off each other, and I sit next to her on the bed, grateful she's alive and home.

Dark Ink is still in Kat's house, too. Their album is complete, and I've listened to it more than once. It's got a good sound. Dave thinks it'll be a best seller and although I'm grateful to them and everyone else for staying, it's time for them to leave.

The shooting has made the entire town come together. I've had more of the locals out here than ever before. Everyone gets patted down, which no one seems to mind. It's like they need to see Kat in the flesh to make sure she's okay.

Kissing Kat on the side of her head, I back out of our bedroom and go downstairs and outside to the deck. The sun is out, so I put my feet up on the railing, enjoying my cup of coffee. My eyes are closed, and I hear the back door slide as someone's heavy footsteps walk toward me.

"Good morning, Dane, how is our brawny biker doing today?"

"Truth, how many times do I have to tell you *not* to call me a fucking biker?" I open one eye and stare at him.

"Pfft, you love it," he says derisively.

Opening eyes, I turn my head toward him. "How's the arm?"

Truth got shot in the arm at the reception. He saw a shooter coming toward Rosie, and he pushed her out of the way, and took a bullet to his upper arm for his efforts. Unfortunately, he faints at the sight of blood, and when he looked at his arm, he went down, hitting his head in the process. Rosie thought he was dead. They've been joined at the hip ever since. She's good for him. He's not such a pain in the ass with her around. At the end of next week, he's going home, and Rosie is going with him.

"Still hurts like a bitch sometimes, but it's better," he says. "How are you feeling about the possibility of Kat going back on the road?"

"Not going to happen for at least another year, then I'll deal. It's her call. If she really wants to do it, I'm not going to stop her, but I *will* be with her twenty-four-seven."

"I'm surprised." Truth leans against the railing, crossing his arms. "Thought you'd have her tied up and away from the world forever."

"Oh, I would like to, but then I'd lose her. We have stuff to work out, and I'm not saying I won't be an overprotective dick, but I love her too much not to let her be her. It's one of the things I liked about her before we even met… her music."

"*Our* music," replies Truth.

I nod and stand. "Yeah, that. I'm going into town. When she wants to come downstairs, make her take the elevator. I'll be able to tell if she walks down three fucking flights of stairs, and I *will* make you pay for it."

"You know we let her come downstairs when you're not home?"

"Of course, I fucking know! The elevator, Truth, get me?" I say sternly.

"Yeah, Dane, got you." He grins. "Hey, if you see Rosie upstairs, tell her I'm here, yeah?"

I give him a thumbs up and walk inside, leaving my mug on the kitchen counter as I go. Walking into our bedroom, Kat is sitting on her chaise lounge, and Curtis is lying on our bed with Jasmin. My hands are on my hips, and I glare at them.

Kat's hand lands on my arm as she stands next to me. "Don't be mad, honey, it's wash-the-sheets-day, anyway. Adelynn will be out later to do the washing for me. But you know I think I can do it myself."

She smiles at me, and I know I'm the luckiest man in the world. Bending, I pick her up, one hand under her knees, the other supporting her back, and place her back on the chaise lounge. Her face clouds over, and she glares at me.

"Nope, not going to happen. When you can bend without groaning, I'll let you... yes, *let you*... do chores around the house. Until then, you *will* take it easy." I kiss her on the lips. "I have to go into town. *Do not* overdo it. I need to see Jonas, and the sheriff wants a word."

"Okay, babe, I'll be good," she mutters.

I laugh at her, and she scowls at me. "I have no doubt you'll ignore me, but if you overdo it and hurt yourself, it impacts me."

"How does it impact you?" Jasmin asks, a small frown on her face.

I grin at her. "We're newlyweds." I turn back to Kat and kiss her again. "See you soon."

Dirt is with me on the ride into Tourmaline. We're going to visit Jonas and Kade will meet us there.

As we drive down his driveway, Addy drives past us, waving, and doesn't stop. Jonas says she's been having nightmares since the shootings.

Who hasn't?

I climb off my bike and I see Kade is already here. The front door to Jonas' home opens, and he walks out with Kade following him.

"Hey, Prez! Dirt, how the fuck are you?" he calls out.

I shake his hand. "I'm good, man."

"When are you coming back to manage the fucking garage? I've had enough of it! Fucking customers!" whines Dirt.

We all laugh, and Jonas asks, "Too early for beers?"

"Fuck, no!" Dirt walks inside the house and straight to the refrigerator at the back of the house.

I shrug at Jonas, who simply shakes his head in return.

Dirt pulls out a six-pack and hands us each one. "It's never too early for beer."

"How's the shoulder?" I turn to face Jonas.

"Aches a little, but nothing to worry about." He subconsciously rubs the spot where he was shot.

I pin Kade with a look. "How did you go, my brother? Did you find the money?"

Since Fith's death, we've been looking for the one point five million dollars he kept from the club when he ran guns out of Tourmaline. His last word was 'loft,' and I assumed he meant an actual fucking loft. I had no idea he had built a memorial to Kat's ma on the Lower Oconee Fire Trail. Apparently, it was their inside joke. They would meet at the L.O.F.T. He built a small frame only three feet high with Ms. Saunders' name, the date she was born, and the date she died on it. Underneath was a cemented compartment containing the money. It was the perfect hiding spot. The trail doesn't get used often, so no one questioned a memorial to a woman who supported a lot of the town with employment.

To get us out of the gun-running business, I had

Kade invest the money in a real estate deal near the Miami coast. The man who's running the deal for us, our frontman, was nervous, and I worried he'd bail.

We've been slowly investing in small amounts, but a large payment of two hundred and fifty thousand dollars was required, and I had Kade take it to him.

"All went smoothly. We're good, Prez."

I nod at Kade, who blames himself for the Minions attacking us on my wedding day. He's done everything within his power to make it up to the MC and me. It wasn't his fault. It was just one of those things. The upside to it is the Minions of Death scattered to the wind, afraid of retaliation, and we took over their businesses and turf. The Pink Pussy is making a profit, and the girls no longer have to service the clients if they don't want to.

I finish my beer, and we shoot the breeze for half an hour, then Dirt and I go in search of the sheriff.

We ride up Main Street and park in front of the sheriff's office. Things have almost gone back to normal, and the sheriff and I appear to be on good terms. He's not a bad guy. We're on two sides of the law, and he lost a man in the shootings—Deputy Billy Barrett.

Walking up to the counter, Billy's replacement says, "Sheriff is expecting you, go on through to his office."

We're in our colors and walk through the bullpen toward the sheriff's office. I knock once, and the door flies open. He looks unusually happy as he motions for us to come inside and sit down.

"Dane, Dirt, you both look good. How's Kat?" He leans back in his seat and entwines his hands on his stomach.

"She's getting stronger every day. You should come out for a visit. She'd like it," I reply.

"I will then. Next week?"

"Whenever you can make time."

Silence fills the void, and Dirt asks, "Is there a reason we're here, Sheriff?"

The smile on his face develops into a full-blown grin. "Sure is. Do you know Mrs. Morris? She lives behind Main Street near the intersection of Bluebell and High Street."

I shake my head as does Dirt. "She doesn't ring a bell. Why, Sheriff?" I ask.

"She's been complaining for weeks about a smell coming from the house next door. She's always complaining about her neighbor, though, you know her, Stella Faulks?" We nod. "Well, I finally went to see what all the fuss was about, and you'll never guess what I found."

He looks so pleased with himself, but I don't enjoy guessing games. "For fuck's sake, Carlos, what did you find?"

"The rotting corpse of..." he pauses, "... Gareth Goodman."

TO BE CONTINUED

If you liked this story,
you can continue with book 4:

The Savage Angels MC Series
Motorcycle Club Romance
Savage Stalker Book 1
Savage Fire Book 2
Savage Town Book 3
Savage Lover Book 4
Savage Sacrifice Book 5
Savage Rebel (Novella) Book 6
Savage Lies Book 7
Savage Life Book 8
Savage Christmas (Novella) Book 9

The MacKenny Brothers Series
An MC/Band of Brothers Romance
Spark Book 1
Spark of Vengeance Book 2
Spark of Hope Book 3
Spark of Deception Book 4
Spark of Time Book 5
Spark of Redemption Book 6

Kathleen Kelly

Tackling Romance Series
A Sports Romance
Tackling Love Book 1
Tackling Life Book 2

Standalones
Wraith
Cardinal: The Affinity Chronicles Book One
Crude Possession: Crude Souls MC
Snake's Revenge: Gritty Devils MC

ACKNOWLEDGMENTS

To you, the Reader – THANK YOU!
I am forever grateful that out of all the books available to you, you chose to buy one of mine.
I really hope you enjoy it or them.
If you would like to contact me, I am available – EVERYWHERE – so please find me.

To the Bloggers and everyone who helped promote me on FB – THANK YOU from the bottom of my heart!! If you all didn't help get my name out there, I doubt I would have sold one book, let alone the amount I have.

To Kelly's Angels, you ladies make me laugh! I love your comments and the pictures you post for me in our group. THANK YOU! I appreciate the shares, the pimping and, most importantly, the reviews. Without reviews, we Authors don't survive for long.

To those that don't know me, I do not ask for 5-star reviews, I ask for **honest** reviews.

The last time I did this, we were at 100. Now we are over 200. Actually, we are at 248!

Please forgive me for not putting all of your names down.

Please keep up the good work, and if you ever need anything, you all know where to find me.

CONNECT WITH ME ONLINE

Check these links for more books from
Author Kathleen Kelly

READER GROUP

Want access to fun, prizes and sneak peeks?
Join my Facebook Reader Group.
https://bit.ly/32X17pv

NEWSLETTER

Want to see what's next?
Sign up for my Newsletter.
https://www.subscribepage.com/kathleenkellyauthor

BOOKBUB

Connect with me on Bookbub.
https://www.bookbub.com/authors/kathleen-kelly

Kathleen Kelly

GOODREADS
Add my books to your TBR list
on my Goodreads profile.
http://bit.ly/1xsOGxk

AMAZON
Buy my books from my Amazon profile.
https://amzn.to/2JCUT6q

WEBSITE
https://kathleenkellyauthor.com/

TWITTER
https://twitter.com/kkellyauthor

INSTAGRAM
https://instagram.com/kathleenkellyauthor

EMAIL
kathleenkellyauthor@gmail.com

FACEBOOK
https://bit.ly/36jlaQV

ABOUT THE AUTHOR

Kathleen Kelly was born in Penrith, NSW, Australia. When she was four, her family moved to Brisbane, QLD, Australia. Although born in NSW, she considers herself a QUEENSLANDER!

She married her childhood sweetheart, and they live in Toowoomba.

Kathleen enjoys writing contemporary romance novels with a little bit of steam. She draws her inspiration from family, friends, and the people around her. She can often be found in cafes writing and observing the locals.

If you have any questions about her novels or would like to ask Kathleen a question, she can be contacted via e-mail:
kathleenkellyauthor@gmail.com

or she can be found on Facebook. She loves to be contacted by those who love her books.

Printed in Great Britain
by Amazon